Phoenix

Book One of The Stardust Series

Autumn Reed & Julia Clarke

ISBN: 9781519076663

Chasing Answers

I can't live like this anymore. I repeated the mantra in my head over and over as my feet pounded against the earth.

On a typical day, running was the ideal way to clear my mind and body of stress. But today, the result was quite the opposite. Somehow the chaos in my head fueled my body, and I felt powerful rather than relaxed. I continued down the familiar path and almost laughed at my unexpected burst of energy. Although I ran almost every day when the weather permitted, I didn't think I had ever felt this alive during a run.

The beat of the music playing on my iPod changed, and the scenery started passing by more quickly. Without meaning to, my steps began to keep time with the music as I got lost in my thoughts.

For months, I had been anticipating and dreading this day in equal measure. But now that it had arrived, I was ready to meet it head on. Today I would—finally—stop waiting for answers and start chasing them instead. Oh yeah, and it was also my eighteenth birthday.

My dad, as much as I loved him, had been keeping secrets for most of my life. I knew that my mom was killed in a car accident when I was six. I knew that after her death, my dad moved us to a secluded home hidden in the mountains. And, I knew that he believed it wasn't safe for us to venture out beyond our little corner of the world.

Dad refused to tell me anything else about our past despite my persistent inquiries. Eventually, he agreed to answer all of my questions after I turned eighteen. I somehow managed to stay completely silent on the issue for years now, waiting patiently to reach that all important birthday.

While I was sure he didn't anticipate that I would actually confront him today, I had no intention of letting it go for even one more day. Whatever happened twelve years ago to drive us into hiding had affected my entire existence. Dad's obsession with keeping me safe had kept me sheltered and socially isolated for too long.

Despite my dad's fierce overprotection, I wanted to believe he did his best under the circumstances, whatever they may be. I just couldn't help but wonder if he had taken things too far. Part of me almost hoped that there was some dramatic explanation for our lifestyle, something that would justify all these years of solitude.

Sweat dripped down my forehead, distracting me from my dad's many secrets. Since I was reaching the cool down stage of my run, I slowed to a jog and took in the familiar California landscape. I inhaled the crisp mountain air and basked in the comforting scent of sagebrush intermingled with pine.

Seclusion did have one thing going for it: the view. Our house was located in a valley in the eastern Sierra Nevada mountain range, almost to the Nevada border. The terrain varied from flat to hilly to mountainous. The vegetation was sparse in areas, somehow enhancing the beauty of the surrounding mountains.

Our stretch of the valley was fairly remote and very peaceful. I was more likely to see deer than another human anytime I went outdoors. The closest house was almost a half-mile down a barely two-lane dirt road. Jessica, my one and only friend, lived there with her mom until she went off to college in Las Vegas last year.

After finishing what turned out to be a very satisfying run, I headed to the bathroom for a relaxing shower. I took my time washing and then drying my long, wavy hair. Dad always said that I had his hazel eyes and my mom's auburn hair; like hers, my hair was mostly brown with a glimmer of red in certain light.

Even though I didn't normally wear much make up, I added a light layer of mascara and pink lip gloss and called it good. Before leaving the bathroom, I stared at my eyes in the mirror, hoping to somehow discover new wisdom and experience shining from their depths. Instead, I found the same old Haley peering back at me. I didn't know why I expected to notice a change in my appearance. It was not as if I was going to magically transform from an innocent seventeen-year-old girl into a sophisticated woman overnight. Today may mark my first day of adulthood, but I knew that I was no more worldly than I was yesterday.

I walked down the hallway Dad insisted on using as our personal art gallery to showcase my paintings and sketches. Arriving at my bedroom, I examined the contents of my closet for a few moments. Because of my reclusive lifestyle, I didn't have much of a reason to buy dressy clothes. Most of the time, I stuck to shorts or jeans and casual tops. Thankfully, Jessica sent me a new dress for my birthday, and I knew it was the perfect choice for tonight.

After I finished zipping up the dress, I considered my reflection in the full-length mirror once again. The style of the dress was simple but flattering. It had wide straps, a scoop neckline, and was fitted through the waist, punctuated by a black bow before subtly flaring out. The hem rested a few inches above my knees, showing off my calves, toned from running. It was the type of dress that almost made me want to spin around and around just to watch it twirl.

While the fit of the dress was exquisite, it was the color that made me really love it. The material was the perfect shade of sapphire blue, my favorite color. Peering at myself, I realized that I might not have totally transformed overnight, but I did feel like something was different today. For the first time since I could remember, I felt myself buzzing with excitement and maybe even a little hope.

* * *

Late afternoon, I was finishing the last page of my book when my dad returned from work. He was home earlier than normal but still covered in a layer of sweat and dirt. He set down his heavy gear with a thunk. I heard a note of happy surprise in his voice. "Happy birthday, Haley. You look beautiful."

I felt my cheeks tint slightly and smiled. "Thanks. Jessica sent me this dress for my birthday."

He laughed. "I can always count on her to buy you something girly. Good thing too, since we're going somewhere special for dinner this evening." His delighted expression gave away that he had something up his sleeve.

"We really don't have to do anything special. You know I'm happy to eat at the café." Although my dad made enough to take care of us, we didn't live extravagantly, and I hated the thought of him spending much money on me. Usually we went to a cute café a few towns over for special occasions, and I had expected the same tonight.

Dad gave me a stern look. "Haley, you only turn eighteen once. I've had this planned for months, so just accept it. We're going to stop by the library and then go out to a nice dinner, and you're going to enjoy yourself." When I didn't respond at first, he urged, "Okay?"

I sighed. "Okay."

His smile returned. "Good. Give me a few minutes. I need to take a quick shower and change clothes."

While he showered, I rifled through the mail. It was mostly a superficial chore since nothing ever came other than bills or junk mail. "Ready, Haley?" he called from the other room.

I answered, "Yes," as I grabbed my stack of library books and purse.

Our gravel driveway crunched underfoot, and I stole a sideways glance at my dad as we neared the truck. Used to his daily uniform of jeans and plaid button-down shirts, it was nice to see him dressed up. His dark brown hair was clean and cropped short, and he had shaved, removing his usual scruff. After a summer outside, his normally tan skin had turned an even deeper shade of golden-bronze, and his hazel eyes danced with anticipation.

Once we were on the road, Dad had me laughing as he told me about a tourist who fell in the lake. He never shared anything about his career before moving to the mountains, but I had no doubt that he wasn't always a fishing and snowmobiling guide. Even though he never complained about his job, I knew that it must fail to stimulate him intellectually. Nevertheless, he always had an anecdote ready at the end of each day.

The rest of the drive was spent in companionable silence as we drove to Minden, Nevada, a small town of about three thousand people. Although our address claimed the even smaller Coleville as home, we never stopped in the actual town—not that there was much of a town to speak of. It basically consisted of a couple of restaurants, a few small businesses, and a high school.

Dad insisted that it was almost impossible to stay invisible in a small town, but he had managed to keep my existence a secret for the last twelve years. He kept a low profile himself and developed a reputation as a reclusive bachelor who valued his privacy. The few times someone spotted me and questioned him, he said that his sister and niece were visiting. Amazingly, the lie had worked thus far, so apparently it wasn't completely impossible.

Since visiting Coleville wasn't an option, we usually traveled over the state line into Nevada for all of our shopping and dining. When we pulled up next to the curb at the library, he stopped and looked over at me. "I'll be back in thirty minutes. You have your phone in case you need me. Keep to yourself and I'll see you soon." He winked and I nodded my head. Knowing that I didn't have much time, I hopped out of the truck with my overflowing book tote and hurried inside.

Entering the library, the familiar scents of musty old books and hand sanitizer greeted me as my eyes adjusted to the dim light. Not surprisingly, the building was mostly empty. Apart from the faint clicks of typing and the occasional rustle of pages or shuffling of feet, it was quiet.

Even if my activities weren't so restricted, I thought that the library would still be one of my favorite places. The library's exterior wasn't anything special; it just looked like a generic city building. But as soon as I walked in the doors, the possibilities were endless. I could travel around the world or back in time to ancient civilizations. I could solve a mystery or fall in love. These adventures may have only happened in the books I read, but I would have been lost without them.

Traversing the library, my skirt swished lightly as I made my way to the shelves of books. I quickly immersed myself in finding those on my list and searching for new treasures to explore. The librarians always teased me for maxing out the number of library books I could check out. This visit was unlikely to be an exception.

About twenty minutes later, I was finally satisfied with my selections. Right before I headed back to the front to check out, I remembered to grab Roman Holiday and Charade on DVD. Although I had already seen both, I was making my way back through all of the Audrey Hepburn movies available at the library, and these were the last two on my list.

Since my thirty minutes were almost up, I hastily turned back toward the circulation desk and abruptly collided with something solid. My books soared into the air as I teetered on my feet, struggling to maintain my balance. Helpless to stop the chain of events, I cringed when the books crashed to the floor, shattering the silence. I could feel the heat rising to my face as I turned a deep shade of red.

Crouching quickly to collect the books, my attention was caught by two pale blue eyes. My blush deepened, and I focused intently on the books, murmuring, "I'm sorry. I wasn't paying attention to where I was going."

The boy with the blue eyes quietly responded, "It was all my fault. Let me help you."

We gathered the books in awkward silence, the smell of cedar tickling my nose at his nearness. When he gingerly handed me the rest of my books, I could see the strong muscles of his forearms flex. There was a whisper of touch between our hands, and the contact made my heart flutter.

His smile was friendly with a dimple, and I smiled sheepishly in return. "You're interested in codes?" he whispered. I detected an undercurrent of enthusiasm as he indicated the book on top of the stack titled, *The Codebreakers: The Comprehensive History of Secret Communication from Ancient Times to the Internet.* I nodded; my tongue felt sluggish, and I wasn't sure what else to say.

"You must like reading. You have quite a few books." He was silent for a moment, and I was struck by his smooth jaw line. His shoulders were noticeably muscular beneath the fabric of his blue and gray raglan T-shirt. I should have been intimidated by his obvious strength and height, but I found something about him reassuring.

I realized he was awaiting some kind of response from me. "I'm homeschooled." It was the best I could manage before regretting telling him too much.

His short golden blond hair glimmered under the fluorescent lights as he gently shook his head. "Wow, homeschooled. I would have missed my friends and the swim team if I was homeschooled." He must have been about my age, but he looked slightly older. I felt his crystal blue eyes patiently watching me.

"I guess you can't really miss something you've never had." I smiled nervously as I shrugged my shoulders.

He chuckled softly and shifted his weight while shoving a hand in the pocket of his jeans. I felt like he could read my thoughts, and I was afraid he would figure out how nervous I was.

Sadly, this was the longest conversation I'd ever had with a boy my age. Because of my dad's strict rules, my life was mostly solitary. Sure, I talked with my dad or Jessica and occasionally librarians and shopkeepers on our trips to town twice a month. But this was different. I smiled inwardly; I was pretty sure this didn't qualify as "keeping my head down."

He stopped chuckling. "Wait, you mean you've never gone to a real school?" he whispered in a more serious tone.

"Nope. My dad has homeschooled me since we moved here when I was six." *Why am I admitting this? First I can't speak and now I can't help but answer. And why does he care? He must think I am a freak for being homeschooled my whole life.*

His mouth opened to reveal his surprise, and he tried to hide it quickly. Feeling uncomfortable, I looked down, feigning extreme interest in the floor. There was a pause as he hesitated momentarily. "What grade would you be in anyway?"

Before I could stop myself, I responded, "I just turned eighteen, but I finished my high school curriculum a few years ago and now study whatever I choose." Did that sound like I was bragging? Why was I bragging to this stranger?

His eyebrow lifted as his lips twisted to reveal a surprised smile. "Like codebreaking," he whispered conspiratorially.

My books were getting heavy, and I shifted to relieve the weight from my forearm that had fallen asleep. When he extended a hand to assist me, I felt a twinge of panic at the thought that my dad would return soon. If it was up to me, I'd stay and talk to the cute guy all day. But Dad couldn't find out about this conversation. I had already taken too much of a risk by lingering, not to mention the things I had told him.

I shook my head and smiled. "Thanks, but I better get going."

He reached up and rubbed the back of his head with his hand. "Hope to see you around. Sorry I knocked over your books!"

With one last small smile, I quickly made my way to the circulation desk and flushed in embarrassment once I realized how overdressed I was for the library. While the dress Jessica gave me had a modest neckline, it left my shoulders bare and revealed a hint of cleavage. I tried not to dwell on it; at least I looked pretty when I literally ran into the cutest guy I had ever seen.

As the librarian leisurely scanned each book, I cast a nervous glance at the clock. I tried to conceal my impatience; my dad would be pulling up any moment, and I needed to speed things up. Considering I was always on time, I didn't want him to worry or come in to the library.

With perfect timing, I exited the library as Dad pulled up. It was time for dinner, and hopefully, some answers.

Past, Presents, & Future

Hopping into the truck, I playfully asked Dad, "Where to?"

He smiled but shook his head. "It's a surprise, kiddo. I'm not telling. We'll be there in about twenty minutes."

I figured I wouldn't get any more clues from him, and my mind was already a jumble of thoughts as I replayed the scene in the library on an endless loop in my head. I knew that I was probably just obsessing over my run-in with the blue-eyed stranger because I didn't have any other experiences to compare it to. But, I honestly felt like we had an instant connection. He seemed quiet but friendly, not to mention attractive.

Staring out the window at the passing scenery, I realized that we were traveling in the opposite direction of what I expected. Instead of heading to a restaurant in Minden, Dad was driving west on Highway 207 toward Lake Tahoe. We rarely ventured out this direction, and this section of the road was new to me.

"Are you really not going to tell me where we're going? We've never even gone this way."

Dad's laugh echoed in the quiet cabin of the truck. "Haley, I love your inquisitive mind, but sometimes it really is okay to be surprised."

With a playful tone, I responded, "You know, it is my birthday. Aren't you supposed to cater to my every whim? You're a terrible father. Really, just awful."

Ignoring me, he turned the volume up on the radio before glancing over at me. "Did you say something?"

Shaking my head, I turned to the window to soak up the scenery. The mountains rose on one side while the other presented a valley dotted with homes and landscape much like our own. As we traveled further from Minden, the two-lane road became narrow and windy. Other than occasional turnouts, there were few roads that intersected it. The pine trees became denser and the cliffs steeper. It was difficult to gauge where we were and where we headed.

The road continued to wind, and at some point we stopped climbing so much. Every so often I noticed passing houses hidden in the trees until we finally approached a small town complete with ski resorts and a casino. Assuming our destination must be near, I was surprised when Dad bypassed the center of town.

Not long after, he turned onto a side street with a gated entrance and a guard shack. A variety of ornamental plants surrounded a large, stylized log topped with "Edgewood" in thick metal letters. After passing through the gate, our speed slowed and the scenery subtly shifted to a more manicured look. We passed gently rolling hills, pristine green grass, and a landscape peppered with trees.

The parking lot overlooked a beautiful lake with a large chateau-style clubhouse perched on the edge of the water. Reminiscent of a chalet, it had a slanted roof line and multiple A-frame windows that jutted out. The structure was mostly glass with wood support beams accented by stone.

The natural simplicity of the building's design only served to augment its opulence. Set in the middle of the magnificent surroundings, the many faceted glass windows made it look like a jewel. I was speechless.

We strolled into the clubhouse and immediately entered a sizable room. Guests weaved their way through the lobby to their various destinations. Some were dressed in casual golf attire while others wore suits with ties or colorful dresses. The wood plank ceiling and oversized furniture placed throughout created an effect that was both impressive and inviting. Large floral arrangements gently perfumed the air as we made our way to the restaurant.

The restaurant had immense glass windows that stretched from the floor to the dramatic vaulted ceiling, showcasing the magnificent scenery. A medley of aromas wafted tantalizingly through the air. As we followed the host to our reserved table, I was suddenly more grateful than ever to Jessica for her gift. The overall grandeur of the setting combined with the spotless white tablecloths and elegant china deserved no less than a beautiful dress.

Our table was located right next to the windows, and we had arrived in time to watch the sun set. The mountains beyond were reflected on the lake's glass-like surface as the sun dipped lower in the sky. The host pulled out a chair and indicated I should be seated before placing a linen napkin in my lap and handing me a menu. I had never been anywhere this nice in my entire life; I was shocked Dad brought me here and hoped we didn't look too out of place.

I opened the cork-bound menu but was too busy scanning my surroundings to focus on the offerings just yet. The dim lighting cast a warm glow on the already picturesque scene. Elegant and well-dressed couples and families sat around tables topped with water glasses, a candle, and a vase with delicate white roses. The restaurant was fairly busy, and there was a hushed murmur as people conversed, clinked glasses, and ate their meals.

I felt my dad's eyes on me while I drank in the scene. I sensed that he was pleased with my reaction. The entire experience was overwhelming, and I so wanted to enjoy every moment of it.

A waiter arrived at the table and took our drink order, reminding me that I still needed to look at the menu. After the waiter flitted away, I perused the options and stopped short when I realized there were no prices listed. *Do they assume we are all regulars and know the price? Or do they just figure price isn't a consideration for most of their guests?* Either way, I now dreaded that it was even more expensive than I originally feared.

Apparently reading my mind, Dad spoke. "Haley. It's your eighteenth birthday and I wanted us to do something memorable. Order whatever you like." I started to protest, but he shook his head firmly, clearly ending any further discussion on the matter. I finally decided on chicken stuffed with dates and cashews, served with yam dumplings and drizzled with a sherry shallot sauce. I assumed it was less expensive than lobster or steak, and it sounded really delicious.

While we waited for the food to arrive, Dad and I made small talk. It was strange, because in that moment I felt both grown up and incredibly unsophisticated all at the same time. Surrounded by people in a nice restaurant, I wondered if this was what "normal" felt like.

The setting sun painted a colorful display as vivid shades of orange contrasted against the deep blue lake. The silhouettes of the mountains and trees were still visible but gradually faded to darkness. I mentally snapped a photograph so that I could paint the breathtaking scene tomorrow.

As I grew more comfortable in the unusual surroundings, questions began to creep into my mind. I could tell my dad put some effort into planning the evening, and I didn't want to ruin it with questions about the past. But I also didn't think I would be able to make it through an entire dinner without blurting out at least a question or two. I started trying to figure out how to confront him about our past and my future.

Out of the corner of my eye, I noticed him reach for something in the interior pocket of his suit jacket. Before I could see what the item was, he hid it from my view. He looked me in the eye, and I sensed he was struggling with his emotions. "Haley, I can't believe you're turning eighteen. I will always see you as my little girl, but I'm so proud of the woman you're becoming." I blinked back a tear. Although my dad and I were close, I wasn't used to such emotional statements from him.

He paused and shifted in his seat, running his palm over his short hair before continuing. "I want to give you something special that belonged to your mom." Revealing the item he'd been hiding, he placed a small midnight blue, almost black, leather box on the table in front of me.

I gently untied the delicate white silk ribbon before opening the box. The inside was coated in velvet, and a sapphire and diamond ring sparkled when the light hit it. I gasped as I removed it carefully from the box, admiring the round-cut sapphires that alternated with diamonds connecting all the way around the band.

His tone was solemn. "It was your mother's wedding ring. Sapphire was her favorite stone, and I know it's your favorite color. The sapphires always reminded me of the night sky she loved so much and the diamonds, the stars. Considering sapphire is also your birthstone, today seemed like the perfect time to give you her ring."

I was breathless and unable to respond as I slid the ring on my finger, smiling when it fit perfectly. "I want you to have it, and she would have wanted that too. Wear it and remember how much we love you." The small round stones shimmered in the light, enchanting me with their perfection.

I didn't know if it was a real memory or just my imagination, but in that moment, I could see the beautiful ring on my mom's finger as she placed my tiny hand in her own. Since I didn't have anything else of hers, the ring meant more than any other gift my dad could have possibly given me.

I was still staring at the ring when the waiter arrived with our dinner. With some fanfare, he lifted the domed silver lids off the plates to reveal my chicken entrée and Dad's salmon. After the waiter left the table, I simply said, "Thank you." I was too emotional to express the depth of my gratitude, but I could tell by my dad's affectionate smile that he understood.

Cutting into the chicken, sweet and savory notes filled the air. Each bite was bursting with flavors I had never experienced. Thanks to the pleasant atmosphere and phenomenal food, it felt as though we were floating in a bubble of delight.

Suddenly, my mantra floated back to me. *I can't live like this anymore.* I didn't want to ruin the moment, but I knew Dad wasn't on his guard, and I needed answers. Besides, I figured he opened the door when he gave me my mom's ring.

I eased into the conversation. "It's nice to hear you talk about Mom. You promised to tell me about what happened to her and why we aren't safe."

He gently dabbed his mouth with his napkin, obscuring his expression. I could tell from the shift in his eyes that he was not expecting this and was not pleased. "Let's enjoy your birthday dinner, Haley. We can talk about this later."

I gritted my teeth and smiled, then looked him straight in the eye. "Please, Dad, I've waited long enough. I deserve to know."

He folded his napkin and replaced it in his lap continuing to smooth it despite its heavy starch. I realized I was holding my breath in anticipation. He sighed, "I guess I can't put this off any longer."

Bittersweet

My heart started pounding unnaturally fast. It was hard to believe that my dad was finally going to share what happened after all of these years of not knowing. He glanced quickly around the room and swallowed hard before speaking softly.

"Before you were born, I was a cop in L.A. Your mom and I were happily married for a few years and were thrilled when you came along. Most of my cases up to that point were relatively short, and the danger was minimal. I worked my way up to detective and began handling more difficult cases. I was good at my job but regretted how often it took me away from you and your mom." He took a sip of water and then tugged at his shirt collar.

I saw uncertainty flash in his eyes. "A few months before your mother was killed, my partner and I infiltrated the local branch of a widespread criminal organization. Before going undercover, I took a few precautions, including purchasing our house in Coleville with cash that had been left to me by a distant relative.

My partner and I worked on compiling evidence against several of the high-ranking members of the branch, but we were having trouble gaining access to the type of information that would take them down for good.

As time went on, I felt increasingly uneasy about the situation. Operations within the organization appeared to be running too smoothly and most of the jobs we were included on dealt only with the legal side of the business that they used for cover. I stopped going home at all, unwilling to take a chance that I would be followed. Feeling the need for a backup plan in case something went wrong, I created new identities for each of us—you, me, and your mom—and stashed some extra money in a safe deposit box."

He scratched his hairline and I noticed the perspiration that glistened on his forehead. As he began smoothing his napkin again, I realized that I was gripping my own. Sighing deeply, he continued, "I still don't know what gave us away, but somehow they figured out our real identities. Before we knew about their discovery, several members of the organization lured my partner to a remote location. I wasn't supposed to be there but decided at the last minute to hide in the back of their truck."

He shuddered and quickly sucked in some air. "Not realizing what they had in mind, I was too late. One of the men shot and killed my partner—

who was also my best friend — and I was helpless to react."

I stared at him in shock. In the back of my mind, I guess I always knew that nothing short of tragedy would have caused us to live the way we did. But hearing it out loud made it feel so real . . . and scary.

I silently watched my dad as he tried to pull himself together. He was looking down at his hands and I couldn't tell what he was thinking. But clearly recounting the events of so many years ago was painful for him, and I started to feel guilty for forcing it out of him. I waited until I couldn't stand it anymore. "Then what happened?" I tried to appear reassuring, encouraging him to continue.

He turned back to me and swallowed before quietly continuing his story. "I stayed hidden in the back of the truck, waiting for a chance to escape. During that time, I missed a scheduled rendezvous — where they no doubt intended to kill me — and they became suspicious when I didn't show up. While I was still hiding, I heard the man who had just killed my partner talking to one of his men about his plan to track down your mother. He was hoping that she would lead them to me."

He paused again, longer, and closed his eyes. He took several deep breaths before reopening them. I reached out my hand and placed it on top of his. He looked back at me and then down to our hands on the table. His eyes held a devastation I had never seen before. "Haley, I know that by telling you that your mother died in a car wreck, I was letting you believe that her death was an accident. The car wreck part was true, but it wasn't the full story. Your mom's death wasn't an accident. The car was forced off the road. She was killed because of me. It was my fault."

I sat up straighter and gently squeezed his hand before withdrawing my own. The skin of my palm felt clammy, and I feared what he had to say next. After pausing a moment more, he continued in a quieter voice. Although I knew it was my dad speaking, it sounded like the voice of a stranger.

"Without going into the details, I was able to get away, and I rushed home to you and your mom. We sped out of town and headed toward the mountains. Night was falling as we reached increasingly isolated stretches of road. I was driving, and your mother was in the passenger seat; you were in the back seat behind me. It was well past midnight when I sensed a car following us. I tried to lose them, but they stayed right on our tail."

His voice began to shake. "When we neared a bridge that was in an area with no other traffic, they slammed into the back of our car. I maintained enough control over the car to keep from plummeting off the bridge but still ran off the road into a ditch. We hit a tree on your mother's side of the car, and she was killed instantly. I got you out of the car and made sure it would explode, hoping that everyone would believe we all died in the crash. And then we ran."

He exhaled loudly. As upset as he looked, he also seemed kind of relieved. I didn't even want to imagine how difficult it had been to keep all of that to himself for all of these years.

Having reached the end of the story, he fell silent and I sat unmoving, stunned. Slowly the sounds of the restaurant and the world around us drifted back to me, but we sat there without speaking for a few minutes before the waiter returned for our dessert order. Eager for him to disappear again, we quickly selected the toffee pudding and crème brûlée.

After the waiter whisked away the dessert menus, my dad reached out and rubbed the back of my hand that was resting on the table. "I believed in what I was doing, but it wasn't worth your mom's life. It wasn't worth putting your life in danger. I'm so sorry, Haley."

Over the years, I had considered that on some level my mom's death must have been connected to our move to the mountains. I just didn't expect this type of dramatic outcome.

Still in shock, I tried to fit all the pieces together before finally breaking my silence. "What happened to the criminals? Were they ever caught?"

He looked down at the table and hung his head. "Unfortunately, they're still out there and, I'm guessing, even more powerful than before. I still have my file on them, hoping one day they will be brought to justice."

I considered keeping the question to myself, but I just couldn't. It was the one thing I had to know. "I don't blame you, Dad, but I have to ask. Why did you choose to run? Why not go to the police and turn in the men who did this?"

"That's the clincher, isn't it," he replied. "I could spend the rest of my life trying to justify my decision to run. But it came down to one thing: I had to keep you safe. In that moment, I didn't trust any other person but myself to do so, especially the authorities. I wouldn't be surprised if someone in my department sold us out to the organization.

I had just lost my best friend and my wife that day. I couldn't take the chance with you. And, as hard as it may be to believe, I have never regretted my decision. I know it's been difficult for you, living like this. I'm sorry for that, Haley, I really am. But at least you're alive."

"Is that why we are still in hiding?" I whispered.

He nodded and, out of habit, glanced around the room again. "I wish we were safe after all this time, but something happened a couple weeks ago that you need to know about. I went to a safe deposit box in Sacramento to get your mother's ring. While I was there, someone I used to work with recognized me and called out to me. I ignored him, but I have a feeling it won't matter.

"I'm not telling you this to scare you, but I want you to be extra cautious for a while. If he tells anyone that he saw me, that information could end up in the wrong hands. I have no doubt that there are still plenty of people who would like to know that I'm alive."

He reached into his jacket pocket once again, this time pulling out a small key with the number 738 engraved on it. "Take this and try to keep it with you at all times. If anything happens to me, promise me you will run away and take care of yourself. Don't worry about me, and don't go to the police. When you think it's safe, go to the First National Bank on Post Street in San Francisco. This key will open a safe deposit box that contains items to help you out."

"Dad, do you really think this is necessary?" I didn't want him to think I was blowing off his warning, but I didn't understand his insistence.

"Haley, listen to me. I really hope it's never necessary. But, I have tried to prepare you in case anything ever happens. I need to know that you'll be strong and put yourself first. Understand?" I nodded and he forced a smile. "Good. Let's not talk about this anymore right now. We're supposed to be celebrating. It is your birthday after all."

The waiter arrived with our dessert, effectively squashing further conversation. Before blowing out the candle, I closed my eyes. Numerous wishes came to mind, but I forced myself to narrow it down to one, choosing to focus on my hope for the future. *I wish for an adventure, something unexpected and wonderful.*

Restless

Longing for sleep, I stared at the shadows dancing over my bedroom ceiling. Insomnia wasn't a common problem for me, but there were times when I just couldn't shut off my brain and fall asleep. Considering that my thoughts felt like a thousand butterflies flitting around in my head, tonight was definitely one of those times.

Knowing that no amount of counting sheep would help me, I got out of bed and pulled on a sweatshirt and slip-on shoes. I grabbed a blanket and then tiptoed down the hall and quietly opened the back door. Thanks to years of sneaking out of the house at night, I was able to see where I was going with very little moonlight. I easily maneuvered through the shrubbery until I reached my favorite spot in the yard.

The air was crisp without being too cold. After spreading my blanket over the grass, I lay down on my back and stared at the sky. The smell of dirt mingled with grass soothed me. It was a perfect night for stargazing; the crescent moon provided just a sliver of light in an otherwise midnight-blue sky.

The stars sparkled, reminding me of the diamonds in my mom's ring. I instinctively lifted my hand up to my face, trying to see my beautiful gift in the darkness.

For as long as I could remember, astronomy had been my way of connecting with my mom. She had been a brilliant scientist who worked at NASA's Jet Propulsion Lab. Even though I was so young when she died, I had many poignant memories of her teaching me about the stars.

Staring at the cosmos with her ring on my finger, I felt closer to my mom than I had since she died. As I flipped through my memories like a photo album, I suddenly put together a piece of my history that had been missing for all of these years.

When I was little, I went by the name Kira. After Mom's death, Dad told me that Kira was her nickname for me because it meant "beam of light" and I was her little beam of light. He said that he would start calling me by my real name so that I could keep that special memory of her. My six-year-old self accepted his explanation, and I had considered it a sweet story ever since.

My dad's words about creating new identities for us came back to me then, and the truth hit me with full force. Haley wasn't even my real name; Kira was. It shouldn't have been a big deal after everything my dad shared with me at dinner, but somehow it was the final straw. Even something as fundamental to my person as my name had been a lie. How could I know who I was if I didn't even know my real name?

For the first time in a while, I let my emotions take over. I cried silent tears for my mom and all the years I lost with her. I cried for six-year-old Kira who never had a chance to grow up a normal, happy child. I cried for my dad, who made an impossible decision and lived with the consequences ever since. And I cried for eighteen-year-old Haley, who received the gift of answers on her birthday but now found herself with more questions than ever.

* * *

The sunlight filtered through the window onto my bed, bathing the room in a soft pink light. Its gentle warmth awakened my senses. As I slowly woke up from what must have been a pleasant dream, I heard the gentle sound of leaves rustling and a bird chirping in the distance.

I extended my legs and arms, stretching as I rolled onto my back. It was cool and quiet in the house. I sat up and placed my feet on the rug next to the bed; the wood floor beneath creaked, declaring its age.

My dad already left for the day, off to work before daybreak. Thankful I wouldn't have to face him yet after our talk last night, I climbed out of bed and walked down the hall to the only bathroom in the house. While rinsing my face, I studied myself in the mirror; dark circles under my eyes betrayed my exhaustion.

I shook my head then gently rubbed my eyes to push the sleep away. After stargazing, I must have climbed in bed and fallen asleep at some point, finally worn out. I put on casual shorts and a fitted V-neck T-shirt before walking to the kitchen to make breakfast.

After clearing the mismatched dishes from the table, I washed them by hand in the sink. The house was old but comfortable. Although the wood floor was already pretty clean, I swept it once more. As I quickly folded the quilt and placed it gently over the back of the sofa, it made me wonder. *What was our old house like? Did my mom like cooking?*

My recollections of her and our life before the accident were vague. Sometimes memories that were more like dreams would float through my mind. Now I wondered if they were actual memories from our life before. I pushed the subject out of my mind for the moment and tried to go through the motions of my daily routine.

I walked aimlessly from room to room. Having completed my home school curriculum a few years ago, I had more free time now. Instead of a prescribed regimen, I had the freedom to explore topics that piqued my interest. From navigation and the history of sea travel to art history, my interests were broad. Most recently, I had been delving into the Civil War.

Since I planned to take a walk later in the day, I perused my new library books, finally settling on *Gone With the Wind.* After spending the next hour or so reading, I returned the book to the stack, and *The Codebreakers* caught my eye.

I smiled, reminded of the cute guy at the library and replayed the scene for what felt like the millionth time. I couldn't believe how good-looking he was and that he could seem so nice. Even though it was just yesterday, it already felt like a distant memory or something I had imagined.

I'm sure I'll never see him again, I thought wistfully. *I don't even know his name.* Shaking my head at how silly I was being about a complete stranger, I glanced around the room for something to occupy myself with.

Despite my lack of sleep, I felt restless and decided something creative may help. I grabbed my paint brushes, paint, easel, and canvas and went outside. With few clouds in the sky, the sun played peek-a-boo, casting curious shadows on the mountains. The fresh air and sunshine made it easier to focus.

I circled the house, seeking a comfortable perch, finally settling on one and setting up my supplies. I wanted to get my mental picture of last night's sunset down before it faded away. Raising my hand to paint, a glimmer of light caught my attention. The stones of my mom's, now my, ring glinted in the sun. I sat up straighter on my stool and focused intently on the task at hand, determined to push the swirling thoughts and questions away.

* * *

Late afternoon, with my chores completed, I decided to take a walk to clear my head and stretch my legs. I grabbed my small cross-body bag and added a bottle of water and a snack to the other items I usually carried. I slipped on my favorite canvas flats and locked the door behind me.

Walking in the direction of the mountains, the worn dirt path crunched beneath my feet. My mind and body felt heavy as I slowly made my way toward my favorite escape, hoping to find solace. After walking for twenty minutes or so, the familiar path widened to reveal a small clearing with a majestic old tree. I loved to relax under the huge tree and daydream; something about the place was magical.

I slumped down in the grass against the tree and leaned back against its reassuring trunk. The large branches arched protectively above me, letting sunlight flicker through the leaves. With my feet flat on the ground and my knees bent, I settled in and my gaze clouded.

The dam holding back my thoughts and questions gave out, and I didn't resist any longer. I should have known better than to hope for a dramatic explanation for our peculiar lifestyle. Clearly my request was granted and then some.

Dad was a detective, I thought. *That makes so much sense.* Out of everything he told me the night before, I found his former career the least surprising. A thousand tiny moments with my dad flashed through my mind: teaching me basic self-defense maneuvers and how to shoot; instructing me on how to be aware of my surroundings and quizzing me on my observations; teaching me how to live in the woods with very few supplies.

As fervently as I hoped that nothing would ever happen to him, I was also grateful for all of the practical skills he had taught me over the years. At least now I knew there was a reason for his lessons. If only he hadn't kept the truth from me for so long. I was trying to understand his perspective, but I still wondered why he had been so secretive until now. Did he not trust me?

I clutched at the grass between my fingers. *Is Dad right? Are the criminals behind Mom's death still out there and after him?* Even though I didn't believe he would try to scare me without justification, I hoped that he was just being overly cautious. Surely no one was still looking for him after all of these years.

With all of the thoughts racing through my head, one in particular kept pushing to the front of the line. *What now?* Did Dad really expect us to stay hidden for the rest of our lives? I doubted that he was truly happy in his current situation. He was still attractive and relatively young. And, he obviously had the ability to do something much more rewarding with his time.

Now, more than ever, I feared that he would never be okay with me living the life I wanted. Although he taught me to drive a few years ago, I didn't have a driver's license. I'd never had a job and didn't even have a formal high school diploma. Could I convince him to let me start small now that I'd turned eighteen? I could get a driver's license, a used car, and a job at the library. Would that even be enough for me?

I inhaled slowly and deeply. As much as I longed to experience more of the world, it was difficult to imagine leaving this place for good. It was the only home I remembered, and I inherently drew strength from the beauty and tranquility surrounding me. And yet, I ached for more freedom. The chance to make friends. Go shopping in town without a constant chaperone. Swim in the ocean.

It was times like these that I missed Jessica the most. As my only friend, she had always been my confidante, my shoulder to cry on. Since she moved away for college, we still kept in touch by e-mail. But it wasn't the same. I longed to hear her animated voice and see her mischievous grin. I even missed her incessant nagging for me to loosen up and have fun.

I remained beneath the tree, unmoving, for a long while until a bird crowed in the distance and snapped me out of my dream-like state. Glancing at the time, I realized I had been gone a lot longer than I expected. Knowing Dad would be home soon, I figured I should head back so he wouldn't worry.

Winding down the trail back to the house, anxiety sunk in as I wondered how to approach my dad. *Should I act normal? Should I ask the rest of my questions? Should I force the issue – that I don't want to live in hiding anymore?* I walked lazily, partially out of procrastination and partially from a lack of energy. My limbs were tired and my mind was weary.

Without warning, a loud boom interrupted my thoughts. My body snapped to attention as I tried to determine the source. Straining to listen, I quietly rotated on the spot and realized it had come from the direction of my house.

Knowing Dad would have returned by now, my heart raced wildly. I picked up the pace while I tried to reassure myself that it was probably nothing. Moving quickly, my feet gripped my shoes, and I yanked on my purse strap, forcing it to stop bouncing on my hip.

As the trees thinned closer to the house, the smell of burning filled my nostrils, and smoke was visible in the sky. My mind full of panic, I started sprinting toward the house, the entire time hoping that it wasn't on fire. The temperature continued to rise, and my mouth felt dry. When the house came into view, I could see flames. *Oh my god.*

The area around the house was eerily quiet outside the roar of the fire. I couldn't see or hear any signs of Dad. I wanted to call out to him, but I was breathless and choked with fear. I struggled through the overgrown landscape toward the house, fighting against downed tree limbs and other obstacles. I moved forward blindly, intent on making it to the house as quickly as possible.

Time seemed to slow. My foot caught and I lost control, flying forward to the ground. I landed on my hands and knees, rocks and fragments of wood grinding into my skin. I tried to stand quickly, but my ankle twinged, and I struggled to my feet. *I have to get to the house. I have to find Dad*, I thought.

Forcing myself to ignore the stinging in my legs and palms, I tried to run, but I couldn't move as quickly. With every step, pain radiated from my ankle as I hobbled toward the house. I used the back of my hand to wipe the sweat away from my forehead. The air was thick with haze and smoke; I held my shirt to my nose and mouth, desperate to find a pocket of fresh air.

Flames licked the walls, devouring the house and all our possessions. From within came the crackle and hiss of items as they caved under the extreme temperature. My throat burned, and I fought to suppress a cough. There was no point trying to stem the flow of sweat, my skin first hot and then almost burning as I neared the blaze. *I have to find*

Dad, I repeated over and over to push myself forward.

Suddenly, I was slapped by a wave of heat. I stopped in my tracks, unable to force myself forward. The house and landscape blurred, and a vision of a car on fire appeared in front of my eyes. I could feel my hand reaching out in front of me; I stretched as far as possible but could never quite reach what I wanted. I felt small and helpless and wanted to cry out.

I gasped for air, choking against the oppressive heat. Sinking into an unknown abyss, I screamed for help, but no sound came out of my mouth. Colors swirled in front of my eyes before darkness enveloped me.

Mad for Plaid

A car slammed into the truck from behind. Dad looked over at me and shouted, "Hang on, Haley!" I gripped the seat with both hands as he sped up, practically flying around the curves of the two-lane mountain road.

My body jerked forward when the truck took another hit, this time careening off the edge of the road into a deep ditch. The next thing I knew, I was on the ground outside of the truck as it was engulfed in flames. I could see both of my parents trapped in the truck, screaming for me to help them.

Mom? How did she get in there? I tried with everything I had to reach them, but my body was somehow frozen, unable to do anything but watch while they both disappeared behind the flames.

I could feel myself drifting in and out of consciousness. Thoughts and images streaked through my mind, blurring what was real, what was imagined. I thought I felt hands comforting me at some point. At another, someone gently washed my face. Later, or was it earlier, I sensed it was dark, and I could hear several male voices, faint but nearby.

I tried to force myself to snap out of it, to wake up. *Whose voice is that? How close are they?* Images spun in my head and a wave of confusion washed over me, overpowering me. I was sinking back into darkness.

* * *

I lay in bed with my eyes closed, my eyelids heavy. I felt groggy and disoriented. My body ached and felt wrung out. *Maybe I'm getting sick.*

Inhaling deeply, I noticed scents that were unfamiliar. Even in my bewildered state, I recognized the smell of sheets that were clean but had laid unused in a drawer. Dirt, campfire, and something that I couldn't quite put my finger on mixed in the air.

Why does it smell like coffee? Dad hates coffee.

My skin felt grimy, covered in a film of sweat and dirt. I pried my gritty eyes open and tried to make sense of what was going on. I was in an unfamiliar bed and could just make out the room with only a sliver of moonlight streaming through the uncovered window. From what little I could see, I was in a small bedroom with just a dresser, nightstand, and lamp.

There were two doors, and a sliver of light shone from under the one directly in front of me.

The scent of smoke lingered in the air, and my memory flooded with images of the house fire. I broke out in a cold sweat and my hands started shaking. I had no idea where I was and whether my dad had even made it out of the house okay.

Deciding to investigate, I pushed back the covers and quietly moved to the edge of the bed. I placed my right foot on the ground but immediately pulled it back when pain shot up from my ankle. Glancing down, I was surprised to find an ace bandage wrapped around my obviously swollen ankle.

Certain I wouldn't be able to get to the door without making noise, I moved back to the center of the bed and considered my options. I didn't appear to be in any imminent danger, but there was really no way of knowing who was in the other room. It looked like I might be able to escape out the window, but I wasn't sure whether I could do so quietly, especially with my injury.

I groaned inwardly as the aches all over my body became more and more evident. My head was pounding, and my ankle was throbbing. My knees and palms were scraped and sore, and my throat was burning.

I heard a door close and then someone moving around in the kitchen. Knowing that I was unlikely to escape in this state even if I tried, I decided to get back under the covers and feign sleep. Hopefully whoever was out there would continue to leave me alone while they thought I was sleeping.

As I lay there, my throat began to feel even more parched. I fought the urge to cough, but it became too difficult to suppress, and I eventually gave in. And what started out as a quiet cough quickly turned into loud hacking. *Great. There went that plan.*

A few moments later, I heard footsteps coming toward me and then a soft knock at the door. Too frightened to respond, I pushed my back against the headboard and pulled the covers up to my chin. The knob twisted and the latch was released. My heart was pounding so loud it sounded like a freight train.

The door slowly creaked open, and the room was suddenly filled with light from the hall. I could see only the outline of a very tall man as he cautiously walked into the room. A smooth baritone voice said, "Don't worry; I'm not going to hurt you."

The stranger walked to the bedside table and turned on the lamp before stepping back away from the bed. I stared at his dark blue jeans and green plaid socks while I attempted to get my nerves under control. *Surely a guy wearing plaid socks can't be that bad, right?*

Unable to stall any longer, I finally lifted my head up, and then up some more, to look him in the eye. It took everything in me not to audibly gasp when I saw all of him for the first time. He was incredibly handsome and so tall. My pulse started racing, and I felt myself getting nervous for an entirely new reason.

He had chestnut brown hair that was short on the sides but longer on top and styled to look just a little messy. Behind stylish glasses with black plastic frames, his dark brown eyes appeared concerned and maybe even a little amused. Probably because I was hiding under the blanket like a three-year-old.

I finally gained the courage to ask him who he was, but before I could get the words out, I started coughing again. He handed me a glass of water that he must have brought in the room with him. I accepted the glass but stared down at it with doubt. *I'm guessing the rule against accepting candy from strangers also applies to drinks. What if he's trying to poison me?*

Apparently reading my mind, he chuckled and said, "I promise that it's just water. Do you want me to take a drink first to prove it's okay?" I saw a slight smirk on his face and blushed.

The stranger smiled reassuringly and held out a hand as if to take the glass of water before I started coughing again. Struggling to catch my breath, I lifted the glass to my lips. The cool water splashed down my throat refreshing me.

"Thank you." I had so many questions running through my head, I didn't even know where to start. As the silence became oppressive, I finally asked, "I don't mean to be rude, but who are you and how did I get here? Where am I?"

He moved farther away from me and leaned against the wall, making it easier for me to look up at him. "My name is Ethan. But, the rest is a little more difficult. I know you have questions, but for now just know that I want to help you, I promise. Why don't you take a shower and get cleaned up, and I'll make breakfast. I'm sure you're hungry."

My smoke-scented hair and rumbling stomach couldn't argue with his suggestion. I felt so dirty; if he told me I had to use the garden hose to get clean I would have, gladly. But my head still needed a few answers. "My dad . . ." I couldn't finish my thought, choked up by the possibility that something horrible happened to him.

Ethan's expression turned serious. "What do you remember about what happened?"

Flashes of the night before raced through my mind. It all seemed like a blur now. "Not much. There was an explosion, and I ran toward my house, looking for my dad. I fell and twisted my ankle but got up and kept running. And that's all I remember." I didn't know if I really wanted to hear the answer or not, but I went ahead and asked, "Do you know what happened to my dad?"

Ethan sighed. "As far as I know, he's okay. He got away from the house after the explosion, but I don't know where he is now."

I sat there in silence, relieved that maybe Dad was okay. But, I still had no idea what to do next. There was no way of knowing whether I could trust this man, regardless of how nice he seemed. Suddenly remembering the cell phone in my satchel, I asked, "Do you have my bag? I need to call him." My throat was still raw and dry.

Ethan nodded and left the room. A moment later he returned; my bag looked dirty but mostly intact. I dug around until I found the phone and cringed when I saw the cracked screen. *That's not a good sign.* When I couldn't even get the phone to turn on, I gave up. Clearly my cell phone wouldn't be of any use.

Before I could ask, Ethan pulled a phone from his pocket and handed it to me. "Here, try calling your dad on this. I'll give you some privacy." I watched him leave the room and shut the door softly behind him.

My hands shook as I quickly dialed Dad's cell phone number and waited anxiously for him to answer. My heart sank when I heard, "the number you have dialed is not in service" rather than my dad's voice. What now?

I nervously clutched the blanket. Hoping I had merely dialed the wrong number, but knowing in my heart that I hadn't, I dialed again. Holding my breath, I prayed I would reach Dad this time. My heart started pounding when I got the same message again. Guessing a third attempt was futile, I sank into the bed, anxious about what to do.

There was a light knock on the door. I quickly deleted Dad's phone number from the recent calls log before cautiously responding, "Come in."

Ethan stuck his head in the door. "Did you reach him?"

Not wanting to give too much away, I just shook my head. "Thanks for letting me borrow your phone." He walked the rest of the way into the room and took the phone from my outstretched hand. Needing time alone with my thoughts, I said, "I guess I'll go ahead and take that shower now if you don't mind."

"Of course. The bathroom is the first door on the right. I put a fresh towel and clothes on the counter for you. I don't have any clothes your size, so you'll have to make do with borrowing mine for now. Do you need any help walking?" he asked, glancing at my ankle.

Heat crept up my neck. There was no way I was going to let Ethan help me get to the bathroom. "Um, no thanks. I'll be fine."

"Okay, well, let me know if you change your mind. You can join me in the kitchen when you're finished." He gave me an encouraging smile before walking out of the room.

I watched until his tall form disappeared down the hall and then stood up. I swayed, feeling unsure on my feet and slightly dizzy, before gingerly stepping over to the window to look outside. The sun was just starting to rise, providing enough light to get a peek at my surroundings. Unfortunately, all I could see was dense forest, no civilization in sight, and really no clues as to my location.

With no obvious solutions to my current predicament, I decided I might as well take it one step at a time. For now, I needed a shower and then food. I limped to the bathroom and tried to ignore the sharp pain every time I put pressure on my injured ankle. Thankfully, the bathroom was just a few steps down the hall.

Once I made it to the bathroom, I shut and locked the door before looking around; it was tiny and outdated but clean. A small window let light into the shower, but it was too small to consider climbing through. The linoleum floor creaked gently underfoot, and a row of fluffy peach towels hung behind me.

Catching a glimpse of myself in the mirror, I gasped. I was fairly certain that I had never looked worse in my life. Fragments of leaves and sticks were intertwined in my long hair. Instead of its usual shine and luster, my hair was dusty and tangled. I had streaks of dirt or soot across my cheek and forehead. My whole body was covered in a layer of sweat and grime.

I realized for the first time that I was wearing a men's T-shirt but still had on the now filthy shorts I'd been wearing yesterday. As I undressed, I forced myself not to dwell on the fact that Ethan (or someone else) had changed my shirt. I had bigger problems to deal with. And at least I still had my bra on. I noticed that in addition to the bandage on my ankle, my scrapes had been cleaned and a few even bandaged.

I turned on the faucet, releasing the water and starting the shower. The splashing of the water against the tub was calming. Unable to handle the stinging of hot water on my cuts, I set the water to lukewarm and went about scrubbing myself clean. I grinned at the only soap in the shower: apple-scented body wash. Very manly.

I squeezed shampoo onto my hand and its scent filled the bathroom. Luxuriating in the warm water, I gently massaged my scalp. As I attempted to wash the smoke scent out of my hair, it suddenly occurred to me. My home for the last twelve years just went up in smoke. Literally.

Although we didn't own that much, it was still a blow to realize that everything was gone. I quickly looked down at my right hand and almost cried in relief. At least I still had my mom's ring. As devastating as losing the house and everything in it was, her ring was the only possession that I genuinely treasured.

Seeing my mom's ring took me back to the dream that woke me up this morning. When Dad told me the story about the car wreck that killed my mom, it didn't totally sink in that I was there when it happened. Even though I was only six at the time, I couldn't help but wonder why I didn't remember the traumatic accident and subsequent fire.

Soap washed over one of my cuts, stinging me and bringing me back to my current problems. If I hadn't been so wrapped up in myself, I would have been making dinner when Dad got home yesterday rather than daydreaming in the woods. I would have been there when the fire started, and we never would have gotten separated. What if I never saw him again? I felt a sharp pain in my chest, my anxiety mounting at the thought.

Okay, Haley, you need to focus. Even though you thought he was exaggerating, Dad did warn you that something could happen to him. Considering the timing, there is no way that the explosion at our house was a coincidence. He told you to run and to take care of yourself first. You have to trust him. He knows how to handle himself, which means he's fine. So stop worrying about him for now and concentrate on yourself.

I thought through my current situation logically, trying to make sense of what happened. I knew that I passed out at the fire and was brought to a secluded cabin in the woods. Ethan, a complete stranger, took me in and cared for my injuries. And, my dad apparently got away from the fire but was chased by unidentified men. It wasn't a lot to go on, and my mind warred with whether or not I could trust Ethan.

On one hand, he seemed non-threatening and even concerned about my well-being. And he did allow me to use his phone to attempt to call Dad. On the other hand, he could be working with whoever was after Dad and using me for information or as bait.

Whatever the answer, I wasn't going to find it by staying in the shower all day. I needed to eat something and try to get more information from Ethan. Hopefully I could at least get a better feel for his intentions.

Tangled

I dried off and took inventory of the clothes that Ethan provided: a soft navy T-shirt and light blue and orange plaid Polo boxers. *Okay, someone definitely has a thing for plaid.* Unwilling to put my dirty panties and bra back on, I pulled on the shirt and shorts and looked in the mirror. I couldn't help but smile at how ridiculous I looked in a shirt made for a man who was so much taller than me. I knew I should be embarrassed that I was wearing a stranger's boxers, but I was so thankful for clean clothes that I couldn't bring myself to care.

Without a brush or hair products to help me out, I ran my fingers through my hair, trying to work through as many tangles as possible. Finally deciding it was a hopeless cause, I left my waves alone to dry. I knew I wasn't exactly looking my best, but at least I was clean and smelling like apples instead of smoke and sweat.

I hobbled into the kitchen, taking in my surroundings as I went. The cabin was clean and somewhat spartan. With low ceilings and rough wood floors, it was just as you would expect.

Exploring the rest of it, I realized there wasn't much more to it than the bedroom and bathroom I had already seen.

On the far side of the cozy living room was a wood door that I supposed was the front entrance. A slightly worn-looking couch and chair sat facing pine shelves filled with assorted books and games. Across from the living room, the kitchen flowed into a dining area with a round wooden table and four chairs placed beneath a brass chandelier. Beyond the table, a pair of sliding glass doors led to a large deck outside.

Apart from the necessary essentials and a picture or two on the wall, the place seemed like it was rarely used. The few pieces of furniture looked dated and the air felt stale. Large windows let in natural light that filtered through the trees giving the feeling of being part of the forest. Inside and outside met almost seamlessly.

I hadn't realized how hungry I was until I smelled breakfast. Ethan's back was to me, and I took a few moments to study him. Admiring the way his pale blue polo shirt hugged his broad shoulders and obvious biceps, I wondered how often he found himself cooking breakfast for a girl.

When he turned around, I saw his eyes quickly flick from the top of my head down to my bare toes and back. Self-conscious about standing there in nothing but his boxers and a T-shirt, I crossed my arms over my chest and looked away.

I was surprised when he walked to the table and grabbed a hoodie off the back of one of the chairs before handing it to me. "Here, you look like you could use this." It was red and had the Anaheim Angels logo across the front. Grateful for more clothing, especially since it was cool in the cabin, I thanked him and pulled it over my head. It was big on me but warm and smelled faintly like cedar.

Ethan pulled out a wooden chair for me next to the round table. I sat down awkwardly, trying to avoid putting more pressure than necessary on my ankle. The chair felt sturdy but creaked under my weight. The table was set with plain silverware that was flat and patternless. It felt like the type of silverware you would find at a cheap, roadside diner.

He turned back to the stove. "Almost ready," he said, still facing away from me. Shaking the pan of scrambled eggs with one hand, he calmly ran the other through his chestnut hair. He moved with ease, clearly in his element.

A minute or two later, Ethan set a large, plain plate down in front of me piled high with scrambled eggs, toast, and fruit. "I didn't have a lot of options, so hopefully you like eggs." The steaming breakfast filled my senses with longing.

Before I could respond, my stomach growled loudly. Ethan just laughed. "I'll take that as a yes." He handed me a glass of orange juice and a sealed bottle of over-the-counter pain medication. "Take two with your food to help with your ankle. After breakfast, it needs an ice pack and elevation." I stifled my urge to salute him.

Ethan pulled out a chair and sat down across from me. Despite his size, he moved smoothly, more like an acrobat than a cat. I thanked him and quickly tucked into the savory scrambled eggs and sweet fruit. Perhaps it was my hunger talking, but I was pretty sure this was one of the best breakfasts I had ever tasted.

I had almost cleaned my plate when I felt his eyes on me, and I slowly raised my own. His dark brown eyes betrayed a hint of wonder. I quickly looked down and folded my hands in my lap, embarrassed. I didn't often eat in front of others, and while my dad had taught me manners, I was so consumed by hunger I had forgotten to use them.

He chuckled, "Don't let me stop you. There's more if you're still hungry."

I shook my head. "I'm good. Thank you for the delicious breakfast. And for taking care of my injuries."

He responded with, "No problem."

My hunger mostly satisfied, I picked at the remaining food, contemplating what to say next. Ethan spoke first, breaking the silence. "Feeling better now?" I nodded. I still felt like I had been run over by a train, but the shower and breakfast helped dramatically.

Debating how to broach the subject of my dad, my pulse quickened. Not knowing who Ethan was and what he knew, I needed to tread carefully. "You said you saw my dad get away from the fire?"

The light coming in through the windows glinted on his hair and face. I noticed the shadow of stubble on his jawline. He nodded, his hair shifting slightly with the movement. He looked a few years older than me; I guessed he was in his early to mid-twenties. I was struck again by how handsome he was.

Fiddling with the napkin in my lap, I hoped to keep my voice calm and level. I didn't want to reveal anything more than necessary about me or my dad. Nor did I want to show how nervous he made me. Looking down to keep from staring at his chiseled face, I finally said, "I kind of live in the middle of nowhere. What were you even doing there?"

He answered slowly, as if weighing what he should say. "I was in the area and noticed the smoke. Since I have medical training, I went to the scene to see if I could help."

I internally scoffed at his response. Did he really expect me to believe that he just happened to be in the area? This whole situation was so suspicious, I had difficulty keeping my disbelief hidden. "Can you tell me more about what happened? I don't remember much after realizing the house was on fire." I trailed off, hoping he would fill in the blanks.

I glanced up to find Ethan studying me. "I know you have no reason to believe me, but I promise to tell you the truth even if I can't go into all of the details." Apparently I hadn't masked my reaction as well as I thought.

"I really was in the area with a colleague when your house exploded. We were still several miles away but saw the smoke and immediately headed that direction. Soon after, a truck approached and then sped by with a car right on its tail. Your dad was in the truck, but I don't know who was following him or where he went."

Ethan paused, giving the new information a chance to sink in. I clutched my napkin and tried to keep my face unreadable while my mind whirred, trying to figure out what happened. The obvious answer was that the criminal organization Dad told me about managed to find him. Did they cause the explosion, trying to kill him? If he got away, where was he now? And how did Ethan even know that it was my dad in the truck?

"We didn't know what was going on, so we continued in the direction of the smoke which was billowing in the sky by that point. We searched the outside of the house but didn't see or hear anyone, so I reported the fire to the authorities and left. Chase called and told me that he rescued you and was headed toward the cabin. Since I'm a paramedic, he knew I would be able to help with your injuries.

"When I arrived here, you were unconscious on the bed. But your injuries were pretty minor, and I could easily treat them myself. I checked your breathing and then tended to your ankle and other superficial wounds before leaving you to sleep. Mostly, you just needed rest after such a shock."

I absently twirled my hair around my finger, trying to put all the pieces together. Apparently Chase saved me, but I didn't even know who he was. And if he and Ethan really just wanted to help me, they could have dropped me off at the hospital or called the police. Instead, they brought me to a deserted cabin in the woods. That wasn't normal behavior, even if Ethan was a trained paramedic.

Ethan cleared his throat. "Do you have any idea where your dad might have gone?"

I debated the best response and finally shook my head. Ethan's dark brown eyes met my own and intimated a hidden reserve within. "I want to help you find him." It felt like he was trying to read my mind and simultaneously reassure me.

I tilted my head and crossed my arms. Afraid to utter my thoughts, I settled on a question that was more vague. "Why do you want to help me?"

Ethan sighed and pushed his glasses up on the bridge of his nose. "Look. There's more going on here than I can tell you right now. You're just going to have to trust me."

I felt one eyebrow raise in response. *That was a bold request from someone who was involved in basically kidnapping me.* Yes, I knew I was being slightly dramatic, but I couldn't help it. Even though he seemed well-meaning, I would not hand over my trust so easily. I felt my patience snap, and I let him have it.

"Ethan, I can appreciate that there are things you can't tell me. But, I at least need you to explain why you are involving yourself in my life. And why Chase, whoever that is, decided it was okay to bring me out here. To a one bedroom cabin. In the middle of the woods."

A look of surprise crossed his face during my short rant. And then he started laughing, a smooth, deep laugh that caused goosebumps to crawl up my arms. "You know, I'm happy to see that backbone of yours. You were making this too easy on me."

When I continued to stare at him, he relented. "Okay, here's the deal. Chase is a colleague and friend; actually, that's his hoodie you're wearing. He had the best of intentions. Since he wasn't sure what happened back at your house, he was concerned for your safety and knew that you would be fine here."

The sound of Ethan's chair scraping against the wood floor signaled the end of the conversation. Ethan took my plate, gently brushing my forearm as he did so. Turning toward the sink, he quickly whispered in my ear, his warm breath tickling my skin. "We're the good guys, I promise."

I felt a flutter in my stomach, and my face flushed while thoughts swirled in my mind like clothes in a washing machine. Every word from Ethan was reassuring, and yet, he had repeatedly avoided telling me why he and his friends were so eager to help me. I sighed, distracted by Ethan's alluring touch and promises of good intentions. I still felt confused and wasn't sure what to do next.

The rest of the day was spent idly. Ethan was around but mostly left me to my own devices. At one point when he was outside, I rifled through the only paperwork I could find in the house, none of which named an Ethan or Chase. I discovered the address of the cabin was in Markleeville and felt a tiny glimmer of relief. Although I wasn't very familiar with the small town of Markleeville or the landscape surrounding it, I knew it was only about a half an hour from Coleville. At least I wasn't as far away from home as I'd feared.

After lunch, I spent time outside on the deck reading and surveying my surroundings. Now that I knew my general location, I felt confident that I could find my way into town. But what then? I had a little money in my bag, but not enough to live off of for long. I wanted to ask Ethan more questions but doubted he would give me the answers I was looking for.

What would Dad tell me to do in this situation? I had no doubt he would advise me not to trust the random guy who wouldn't tell me why he was helping me and was obviously hiding things. Dad had already told me not to go to the police. The only logical conclusion was that I should run and make it on my own until I could find him. I sighed, resigned to sticking it out the rest of the day and then escaping after dark. I glanced down at my wrapped ankle, fervently hoping it could handle the long walk through the woods.

* * *

It had been a long day, and I felt no closer to finding my dad than I had this morning. Ethan suggested that we turn in since it was getting late. He insisted I take the bed again, stating that he was fine on the pull-out sofa bed. His kindness and generosity overwhelmed me; I was even feeling a little guilty about my plan to slip out during the night. *And yet, how could I trust him when he seemed so determined to hide his motives from me?*

As I limped toward the bedroom, I heard the front door open behind me. Startled by the unexpected intrusion, I jumped. Glancing quickly at Ethan, I noticed that his eyes had darted toward the door. Turning slowly, I felt my jaw drop; the intruder was the blue-eyed stranger from the library.

Brick Wall

I stared at the ceiling, forcing myself to stay awake. I thought through everything I knew about my dad, the fire, and the boys, seeking answers, seeking inspiration for what to do.

Having convinced myself that I would likely never see the blue-eyed stranger from the library again, Chase's reappearance at the cabin was the last thing I expected. I played our latest conversation over again and again searching for clues, trying to figure out what was really going on.

Initially surprised and excited in spite of myself, I asked, "What are you doing here?"

I saw the corner of his lip twitch upward. "Haley, right? I'm Chase."

"How did you know my name?" I blurted out, not intending to say it aloud.

He shoved both hands in his pockets. "I overhead the librarian call you by your name." I couldn't argue with that explanation. The librarian was one of the few people who actually knew my name and had most likely used it in front of Chase.

I couldn't believe that the two hottest guys I had ever seen were not only in the same room but seemed to know each other. Chase's blond hair and blue eyes contrasted nicely with Ethan's chestnut hair and brown eyes. Both muscular, they were equally breathtaking in their own way, and I could feel my mind wandering as I studied their impressive builds. Focus, Haley!

I looked inquisitively between Ethan and Chase, wondering what was really going on. I seriously doubted it was a coincidence that Chase was at the library, then the fire, and now the cabin. Ethan's face betrayed nothing, while Chase's suggested that he was both bewildered and amused. Suddenly I remembered that I was wearing Ethan's boxers and Chase's over-sized sweatshirt. Being alone with Ethan in this state hadn't bothered me as much as I thought it should, but being with Chase now, I felt slightly awkward about it.

I crossed my arms, attempting to smother how self-conscious I felt. Silence filled the room, creating an awkward void.

Finally, I spoke. "Thanks for rescuing me."

I noticed a twinge of red creep up Chase's neck before he looked down at the floor. "Sure. I mean, you're welcome." He gently kicked the air with one foot.

With my arms still crossed, I pinched some of the fabric of the sweatshirt. "What did you see yesterday? Do you know anything more about my dad?"

Chase looked toward Ethan and I noticed the briefest nod from Ethan. Perhaps I was seeing things, but it seemed like they were silently communicating. Chase took a deep breath.

"When I saw the house burning, I wanted to make sure no one was inside. I didn't see or hear anyone at first. But when I got closer, I saw you laying on the ground, unconscious. When you wouldn't wake up, I carried you to my car." He paused. "I brought you here so Ethan could check out your injuries. I don't know where your dad is, but I wish I did."

As the memory faded, I glanced at the bedroom door. I had been in bed for a few hours, biding my time. I closed my eyes, my ears focused and listening for any sound. *Now's your chance*, I thought. *If you're going to do it, you need to do it now. My pulse quickened*.

I slipped out of the bed as quietly as possible and gently picked up my bag, heavier now with a few extra supplies I had surreptitiously gathered throughout the day. As I threw it over my shoulder, I heard a creak. Freezing, I held my breath, waiting to see if it was just the noise of the cabin or one of the guys moving around. After a few long seconds, I grabbed my canvas shoes and moved toward the window across the room.

I slowly unlatched the window then lifted it as quietly as possible, fearing any sudden sound or movement. Fortunately the drop from the window sill to the ground was only a foot or so, and there were no bushes on this side of the cabin. After making a space wide enough to fit through, I slid through the opening, taking care of my sprained ankle.

The ground depressed gently beneath me as I landed on my feet, well, mostly my one foot. The soil was soft and moist but not so wet as to be muddy. The dampness from the rain the night before lingered, accentuating the scents of the forest; pine, moss, and damp earth mixed in the cool air.

After glancing around to make sure no one was about, I hesitated, debating whether to attempt to close the window. I took a deep breath and didn't exhale until the window rested a few inches above the sill. Crouching near the ground, I paused to reorient myself, and the pine needles shifted under my feet. The waning moon was high overhead by this point, but thanks to the dense trees, the area around the cabin remained dark.

Keeping my body low, I made my way north to the road behind the house. My ankle was aching, but rest and painkillers had helped some; adrenaline helped even more. After putting what felt like a safe distance between myself and the cabin, I paused behind a large tree. Having made it this far, I drew a few breaths to still my beating heart before briefly closing my eyes to recall a dog-eared map of the area that I had found in the cabin earlier in the day.

My goal was to head east to Highway 89 and then figure out my plans from there. Not wanting to get too close to the road and risk discovery, I planned to skirt the creek that ran parallel to the road until I hit the highway. If I was right, it was a little over three miles to Highway 89. Normally three miles would be no big deal, but tonight my progress would be slow, hampered by unfamiliar terrain, the dark, and my injured ankle.

Away from the immediate threat of discovery by Ethan or Chase, I noticed for the first time how cold and dark it was. I was still wearing Ethan's boxers and T-shirt as well as the sweatshirt he had given me that morning, but goosebumps raised on my bare legs. The night was so cool I could almost see my breath.

Burying my nose and mouth into the sweatshirt for warmth, the scent of cedar drifted to my nose, recalling the images of Chase and Ethan. At that moment, I half considered turning around to go back to the cozy cabin. They said they wanted to help me; maybe I should have stayed.

Tempting as the idea may be, I knew I couldn't go back; I had no idea who they really were and I couldn't take the risk to find out. Instead, I headed further north in the direction of the creek. Crossing the small, two-lane road, the pavement felt hard beneath my feet. This far away from town, the houses were few and far between, and with no cars in sight, the forest was quiet.

Occasionally the trees thinned out enough for the moon to filter through, casting long shadows on the ground. When I heard the movement of water over stones, I knew the creek couldn't be far. The air felt more humid and I was calmed by the sound of the flowing water. Once I was close enough to the creek, I turned right to head east toward Highway 89.

Feeling simultaneously tired and on edge, I was startled when an owl hooted nearby. I rolled my eyes at my jumpiness; I had been alone outside at night countless times before. Stay calm, Haley. Telling myself to remain calm and rational was one thing; doing it was another. This was unfamiliar territory, and I felt more alone and afraid than I ever had.

I picked up my pace, my ankle burning in fiery protest to the movement. My heart was beating faster, and I struggled with the terrain, encumbered by the small rocks, pine cones, and fallen branches that littered the ground. My limbs felt rubbery, each step forced and clumsy.

Focused on reaching my destination, I pushed myself to keep moving despite the pain and exhaustion. Time seemed to drag on, and while I knew I was headed in the right direction, I wondered why it was taking so long.

Suddenly I flew forward, falling to the ground. Surprised and slightly winded, I quickly pushed myself off the ground, brushing pine needles and dirt from my shins and palms. Don't stop, Haley. You can do this, I reminded myself, forcing back tears. But the words felt hollow. My life was out of control, and I was frustrated by the situation, by my ankle. Tired and scared, I just wanted to go home to my dad.

I decided to sit down on a log to rest. Shivering, I held myself and tried to rub my arms and bare legs. My mind and body were at war; I knew I had to keep moving, and it would help me stay warm, but I was so tired.

A twig snapped and I practically leapt out of my skin. Clasping my hand over my heart, I took a few deep breaths. *You're just tired, stop being so jumpy.* Straining my ears, I didn't hear anything at first other than the sounds of the forest. My eyes darted around the surrounding area until something caught my attention. Not far away I could see a small light bouncing around in the dark, and my stomach dropped.

The light was too faint to be a car and too small to be anything but a flashlight. My suspicions were confirmed when I saw a large figure approaching. Heart pounding, I ducked out of sight; in my attempt to hide, I lost sight of the light.

I froze, struggling to hear anything that stood out from the usual sounds of the forest. Crouching near the ground, the smell of damp earth intensified. My ankle burned and my leg muscles felt tight, ready to sprint into a run.

I looked around, attempting to see where the light had gone despite my limited viewpoint. I counted to thirty in my head, trying to wait out the figure, hoping it had turned to go a different direction. After a few long moments, I glanced around again and slowly stood up, exhaling quietly.

Feeling lightheaded, I sat back on the log, trying to gather enough strength to continue. Seemingly out of nowhere, a hand appeared in front of me and I heard a gruff voice say, "Here, let me help you."

Without thinking, I reached down and grabbed a fistful of dirt before standing up to fling it at the man's face. Surprised, he growled and reached out an arm. I was too slow to react, and his massive hand closed around my wrist. I was struck by the raw strength and power it contained.

Instinctively, I squatted down into a strong stance then leaned forward with all my strength. I bent my elbow all the way toward him until he was forced to release my wrist. Free from his hold, I stumbled backwards, scarcely avoiding tripping as I fumbled in my bag. My fingers found what I was searching for, and I grasped the corkscrew firmly between my index and middle finger with the point out.

Instead of pursuing me further, the stranger stopped moving and held out his hands, palms up. He sighed, sounding exasperated. "Listen to me, Haley, you can't get anywhere on that ankle and you're clearly worn out." Startled at hearing my name, I stopped dead in my tracks.

I didn't think it was Ethan or Chase, but now I took a better look. His height was close to Chase's, over six feet. While Chase's body was definitely chiseled, it was the streamlined physique of a swimmer. The man before me was built like a brick wall. I wouldn't want to meet him in a dark alley, I thought. *Too late for that*, I laughed darkly to myself.

He stepped into a clearing between trees, allowing what little light there was from the moon to shine on him. I felt my grip on the corkscrew tighten, the handle practically becoming one with my palm. I couldn't make out much about the imposing stranger other than his dark jacket and jeans and hair just light enough to gleam in the moonlight.

Although I didn't know him, he clearly knew me; cold and afraid, my teeth were chattering uncontrollably. He removed his jacket and threw it on the ground near my feet. "Put it on." His gravelly voice said it as an order, not a request. I hesitated for a second, but I was too frozen to argue.

I grabbed the jacket and put it on quickly, grateful for the instant warmth. His body heat lingered, and I caught the scent of leather, gasoline, and spice. I sat silently, wondering what to do or say.

He backed away and slipped his hands in his pockets, making him appear slightly less intimidating. "I'm Knox. Ethan and Chase were really worried when they realized you were gone." I pulled my legs toward my body and wrapped my arms around my knees. *Seriously, who are these guys and what do they want with me?*

Knox paused and I let the air fill with silence. He took a breath, and I could tell he was working to maintain his patience with me. "Look. I know you don't know us. But we do want to help you."

"Why?" I asked, noticing an edge to my voice.

"What if I make you a deal?" I looked up at Knox, waiting for him to continue. "I know Ethan and you have talked, but he hasn't shared much about why the three of us are involved in this mess. If you agree to come back with me, I promise that we will tell you the rest of the story first thing tomorrow."

I wanted to believe him, but I still wasn't sure. But what choice did I have? Outrunning Knox didn't seem like an option even on the best of days. *What would he say if I told him thanks, but no thanks?* Considering he was wandering the forest at night looking for me, it didn't seem likely he would agree. And even if he did, how far was I from the road?

He interrupted my thoughts, rapidly firing his questions in a sharp tone. "What's your plan, Haley? Think you can make it to the highway and then hitchhike somewhere? Do you have any money? A working cell phone? Do you have any idea where your dad is or how to find him?"

My lips tightened and I shook my head, not wanting to listen. I didn't answer, but he was right. There were too many obstacles for me to make it on my own, at least until my ankle healed. And spending time with these guys seemed preferable to other strangers. At least they seemed to know something about my dad and what was going on, even if they may have been the ones that caused it.

Slowly, Knox stepped closer before sitting next to me. He rubbed his brow as if trying to massage away a headache. His voice was deep, but his tone had softened slightly. "I know your dad is missing and you're worried about him. I have a younger brother and I know what it's like to worry about someone you love. I know what it's like to want to protect them."

Despite his tough exterior, he seemed genuine. Through the darkness, I tried to search his face for answers. He appeared to be telling the truth.

I put my head down on my knees and hugged them even tighter to my chest. Overwhelmed, I closed my eyes. The world was spinning, and I wished I could open my eyes and be back in my house with my dad. Where were those ruby slippers when you really needed them? Even as my mind screamed at me not to give in, I heard myself whisper, "Okay."

Apparently that was all he needed, because the next thing I knew, my body was being lifted from the ground. I should have protested, but I honestly didn't want to. Strong arms cradled me against a muscular chest, and I was enveloped with warmth. I felt comforted, safe.

Balancing Act

The smell of bacon lured me out of my deep sleep. Despite the chilly room, I was warm and cozy under the covers. I stretched my legs out of habit and cringed when pain shot through my ankle in response.

The harsh sunlight felt like tiny pinpricks drilling into my head, and my body ached all over. Opening my eyes, I groaned as I realized I was waking up yet again in the cabin. Remembering scenes from the night before, I turned onto my stomach, burrowing into the covers and burying my head under the pillow. *I can't go out there*, I thought. *I can't face them.*

I briefly contemplated another escape attempt before hunger finally got the best of me, and I swung my feet to the floor. Standing up took significant effort; my ankle wobbled and protested against the slightest pressure. As sore as my ankle had been yesterday, today it felt a thousand times worse.

Stumbling through the forest in the dark was a great idea. And what did it even get me? I was back where I started, in more pain, and no closer to finding my dad. At least Knox promised me answers today. Remembering the feel of Knox's arms surrounding me, my skin tingled involuntarily. Hopefully I could avoid that reaction when I saw him in person.

Still wearing Ethan's boxers and Chase's sweatshirt, I ran my fingers through my hair and smoothed my mismatched clothing. I straightened my shoulders, summoning the courage to face whoever was on the other side of the door. Ethan? Chase? Knox? All three? Just thinking about them made my heart beat a little faster.

I crept toward the bedroom door and slowly turned the knob, wanting to stay invisible as long as possible. The smell of bacon intensified and my stomach growled in response. Peeking out, I could see legs hanging over the arm of the couch. *One guy, check.* From the kitchen came sounds of cooking, the faint sizzle of something hitting a hot pan, the light sound of metal clanking against a dish. *Two guys, check.* I drew a deep breath and forced myself to step out from the safety of the bedroom.

I took a few steps before my ankle gave out, and I stumbled forward awkwardly. *Great, so much for staying invisible.* Arms flailing, I attempted to catch my balance while Chase popped up from his seat on the couch and held out a hand, offering to steady me. His smile was warm, and for a moment I felt even more unstable. I clasped my hand on his forearm, grateful for the support, and smiled in return.

Chase led me to the table and pulled out a chair, patiently waiting as I sat down. Glancing around, I wasn't surprised to see Ethan busy at the stove. He wore a navy and pale orange patterned button-down shirt that was rolled up at the sleeves. The top two buttons were undone, providing a glimpse of his powerful chest muscles beneath. With his shirt tucked into his jeans, his brown leather belt accentuated his tapered waistline in contrast to his broad shoulders. His patterned socks made me smile; today's choice was houndstooth. *I wonder if his boxers match.*

"Good morning, sleepy head." His voice was cheerful and I sensed a note of mocking.

"Smells good," I said, ignoring his tone. He quickly plated the breakfast and set a dish in front of me before joining us at the table. I relaxed a little, feeling less awkward about last night. I took a few bites and reminded myself to eat slowly, savoring the flavors as I felt the edge of my hunger start to fade.

Knox suddenly appeared at the sliding glass door to the deck, and I gripped the sides of the chair to steady myself. Chase turned toward me, a concerned look crossing his face.

As Knox slid the door open, Ethan smirked. "Don't worry, Knox doesn't bite."

My mouth felt dry, and I doubted my ability to speak even if I wanted to. In the light of day, Knox was still intimidating. I hadn't been imagining things last night; he really was as solid as a brick wall. He was just a hair shorter than Ethan—who I had gauged was close to six and a half feet tall—but he was much broader, with wide shoulders.

Knox's dark blond hair grazed his cheeks and fell over part of his face. A dark V-neck shirt clung to his chest, covered by a worn, brown leather jacket. Relaxed jeans and motorcycle boots completed the look. If Chase looked like the blond All-American, Knox was the blond bad boy through and through.

Surrounded by Ethan, Chase, and Knox, I was tongue-tied. Pretending to be absorbed in my breakfast, I observed them one by one. They were each remarkable in their own way, but together, the three were almost more than I could take.

I was interrupted from my thoughts by Ethan. "Haley. Earth to Haley. Feeling okay?"

I nodded, lazily swatting away his hand that was reaching out toward my forehead as if to check my temperature. The corner of his lip twitched upward, and his eyes flickered with amusement as he resumed eating. After a few bites, he looked at me. "Speaking of. How is your ankle feeling today?"

I pushed my food around a little before speaking in a quiet voice, still focused on the plate in front of me. "It feels fine, I guess."

He scoffed. "I'm sure it does after walking on it all night. Do you mind if I take a quick look at it?"

"No," I replied, avoiding looking him in the eyes. I felt the most guilty facing Ethan after running away; probably because he had taken care of me and spent so much time with me yesterday. He very gently lifted my leg and rested my foot on his thigh. Inspecting my ankle, he lightly pushed at the swelling before placing my foot back on the ground.

"I think you'll live," he said with a slight smile.

Ethan looked me directly in the eye, his rich brown eyes holding my attention until he finished giving his orders. "Stay off that ankle today, Haley. I mean it. Rest it, ice it, and take the medicine I gave you yesterday. Don't put any weight on it; Chase and Knox will help you get around when you need to. We will have to get you some crutches later."

Before I could respond, Ethan pushed his chair back from the table and headed toward the sink to rinse his dish. I didn't realize he was leaving until he walked to the door, pausing only to grab a brown leather satchel. "I'll see you later. Play nice." He winked at me before closing the door behind him.

I gulped, realizing I was alone with Knox and Chase. Although I didn't know Ethan well, I felt like I knew him better than the other two. We finished our breakfast and Chase asked if I would like to shower. I attempted to get up from the table but felt myself falling back into the chair when my ankle refused to cooperate.

Chase shot me a kind, understanding smile and rose from his chair. "Here, allow me." He pulled out my chair and then held out his hand, palm up. I grasped his forearm, enjoying the warmth of his skin under the golden blond hair and the lean muscles that flexed in response to my touch. Once I was standing, he turned so we walked side-by-side and shifted his weight to bear more of my own.

I felt my cheeks redden at the intimacy and looked toward the floor, letting my hair cover my face. Closing the bathroom door behind him, I found that someone had laid out clean clothes for me on the counter. Thinking back to day I met Chase at the library and what he was wearing, I wondered if the olive-colored raglan shirt belonged to him. With Ethan's affinity for patterns, I would have been surprised if the shirt and solid gray sweat pants were his.

I also noted the addition of conditioner and a comb. *Hmm, was that a hint that my hair was a mess?* I showered quickly, then ran the comb through my hair and put on the clothes. After walking around in Ethan's boxers all day yesterday, I was happy for the sweats even though I had to roll up the waist and hem to keep from tripping on them. I unlocked the door, tentatively wondering what to expect for the day.

As soon as the door was open, Chase was there to meet me. I felt his eyes glance over me and then linger briefly before he quickly looked away. I blushed, wondering if I looked even more ridiculous than I realized. He stepped beside me and attempted to guide me as he had before, allowing me some space and letting me lean on his forearm.

Although my shower had been brief, standing for so long had taken its toll. I started to lose my balance, and Chase reached a broad arm around me, supporting and warming me. He drew my arm up around his shoulder, gently holding on to my waist as he helped me hop across the room. Being so close to him was intoxicating.

A couple of days ago, I would have gone into shock at the contact. But, I could already feel myself getting comfortable with these guys. Well, Chase and Ethan, at least. Chase cleared his throat. "How about the couch so you can put your foot up?" I nodded at his suggestion then quickly regretted it when I saw Knox already sitting on the chair nearby.

After I was settled on the couch, Chase grabbed an ice pack from the freezer. Wrapping it in a towel, he placed it carefully over my ankle. My stomach fluttered and I smiled inwardly, reveling in how sweet and good-looking he was. I hated feeling dependent on anyone, but if it had to be someone, Chase was definitely an attractive option.

Out of the corner of my eye, I saw Knox thread his fingers through his hair, pulling it away from his face. Too curious about him to resist, I turned my head to take a closer look. At least a day's worth of scruff covered his face; it was a slightly darker color than his hair and created the illusion of a shadow. The V-neck T-shirt left little to the imagination, revealing powerful chest muscles beneath its thin fabric. The hint of a tattoo snaked down his formidable bicep. I couldn't make out the design and wished I could see the rest of it. *I wonder if he has any other tattoos?*

My cheeks started to heat at the thought of inspecting Knox's bare skin for more tattoos. Instead, I forced myself to focus on the dark leather bracelet that rested on one wrist. He sat in a relaxed posture, one ankle rested on the opposite knee, focused on his phone.

Suddenly he looked up, catching me before I could look away. Embarrassed, I quickly looked down, acting absorbed in my hands. Chase finally came to join us in the living room. Before he sat down, Chase asked, "Need anything, Haley?"

I shook my head and smiled. "I'm good, thanks." Under my breath I added, "Unless you guys want to give me some answers."

Knox glowered at me. "Answers, huh?" I opened my mouth, surprised he heard my comment. I pressed my lips together tightly, unsure what to do. I felt like a boxer dancing around the ring, waiting for my opponent to throw the first punch.

Gloves Off

Knox continued to watch me, forcing me to return his fiery stare. The air caught in my chest; his striking green eyes were captivating and gazed back at me with an intensity that was unnerving. They were framed on top by broad, arching eyebrows while dark circles cast shadows from fatigue. Distracted momentarily, he caught me off guard with his question. "Why did you run away last night?" His tone was aggressive and I gulped.

Without thinking, I responded. "Why do you think?" My tone came off more defensive than I wanted, but I felt like I was being attacked. I glared at him. "How would you feel if you had lost your home in a fire, didn't know where your family was, and had been taken to a cabin in the woods by strangers?"

Chase shot me a reassuring smile. I wanted to get off to a good start, but Knox was making it difficult. I sighed and decided to ask a basic question. "How do you know each other?"

Knox answered. "We all work together."

Wow, you're really giving me a lot to go on here.

He narrowed his eyes. "Where did you learn that move you pulled on me last night?" Chase sputtered, almost spitting out the water he was sipping.

I felt intimidated by Knox, but there was no way I was going to give him the satisfaction of knowing it. "My dad taught me." If he was going to give me short answers, I was going to give him the same in return. My turn. "What were you all doing in the area and at my house? You obviously don't live in this cabin, so I'm guessing you're not from around here."

Chase stayed silent as if waiting for Knox to answer. Knox's face was unreadable and while I couldn't be sure he was the leader, both Ethan and Chase seemed to defer to him. Whether through fear, respect, or both, I could see why they may hesitate to contest Knox's authority.

"You're right," Knox responded, "We're not from here. The three of us live in Santa Cruz and were in the area for our job." He paused, making me wonder if he was going to stop after that measly explanation. Crossing my arms, I fought the scowl forming on my face.

After a few long moments, Knox continued. "We work in private security and do private investigation on the side. We came to Coleville on assignment . . . and that's where you come in." He paused again. "Haley, we were hired to find your dad."

My pulse started racing. Was he admitting that they were responsible for everything that had happened? Did the guys lead the criminals straight to Dad? I couldn't help but feel disappointed that Chase, Knox, and Ethan were involved in some way. It was the only explanation that made sense and suddenly I wanted to lash out at them.

Chase interrupted. "We were hired to find your dad, but we had nothing to do with the explosion at your house or your Dad's disappearance. We don't know what happened. We want to help you, and we want to figure out what's going on."

I watched Chase's face as he talked. His blue eyes appeared clear and honest. He seemed so sincere, it was almost impossible not to give in and completely trust him then and there.

Knox spoke then, breaking the spell. "You didn't appear to be carrying a flashlight last night; it made it pretty difficult to find you."

I scarcely held in a laugh, surprised by the change of subject. "Oh, good. You know I wasn't trying to be found."

I felt the air in the room lighten. He scratched his chin, and I could hear the short hairs brushing against his fingers. "Did you drop the flashlight at some point?"

I shook my head. "Nope." He seemed to be done interrogating me, at least for the moment.

He stopped scratching his chin. "I'm just trying to figure out how you made it two and a half miles in the dark."

I grinned. "It was simple really, I used my eyes."

Chase laughed, but Knox narrowed his eyes. "There was barely any light from the moon last night. You mean to tell me you can see in the dark?"

"Sort of."

He started laughing, a laugh that was deep and hearty. "You're kidding, right?"

My face felt hot now. "No. I've trained myself to see better in the dark. Most of the time, though, I use a special flashlight with red light that helps preserve my natural night vision." Knox stopped laughing and shook his head.

I furrowed my brow. They had given me some answers, but I still had a lot of questions. I still wanted to know who they were working for. Feeling braver now, I decided to push the issue. "Last night, you promised to tell me the rest of the story. Who hired you to find my dad?"

Knox responded, his voice calm but direct. "I can't tell you that. I can tell you that we did a full background check on our client and didn't find any reason to be suspicious of his intentions. Now that we know men were following your dad and he has disappeared, we are concerned about the possibility that our client is involved."

Knox leaned forward, resting his elbows on his knees. He dipped his head and massaged his temples with his fingers, eyes closed. "Haley, who do you think was chasing your dad?" He sounded tired.

I considered the best way to respond. Knox and Chase obviously knew a lot more than they initially let on; maybe they were still holding back details that would help me find Dad. With escape no longer an option at this point, I realized I may have to give them a little information if I wanted some myself. Besides, if they were working with the criminals, relating part of Dad's backstory probably wouldn't tell them anything new.

My palms felt clammy. I knew providing some information could help, but secrecy and silence were so ingrained in me that any disclosure, however slight, felt like betrayal. I grabbed a pillow from the couch, hugging it tightly. "My knowledge of all of this is very limited; I really only know a few things that my dad told me. Long story short, my dad used to be an undercover cop in Los Angeles."

I paused, debating the best way to relay the story quickly. "About twelve years ago, he and his partner were working undercover with a criminal organization; I don't know any names or details. His partner was murdered after his cover was blown, but Dad was able to get away. We went into hiding and have been living in Coleville ever since."

I'm not sure what I was expecting, but neither Chase nor Knox seemed terribly surprised by this revelation. I hugged the pillow closer, tightening my grip. "As far as I know, our identities and location have remained a secret for all of these years. But, Dad told me that he was spotted a couple of weeks ago in Sacramento by a former colleague, and I'm guessing that's not a coincidence."

I let out a breath, feeling relieved by sharing the story but also drained. I was getting hot and the air in the cabin felt stifling. *I need fresh air.* Forgetting about my ankle, I tried to stand, wanting to head out to the deck. My feet started to give way, and Chase and Knox jumped up simultaneously.

Before I knew it, Knox was standing behind me, his arms supporting me. Chase's face was full of concern. I sighed. "I just wanted to go out to the deck for some fresh air."

I was shocked when Knox lifted me into his arms rather than acting as a crutch like Chase had. Out of instinct, I wrapped my arms around his neck and held on for the short walk to the deck. Chase moved to open the sliding door; the cool, fresh air was soothing and I felt somewhat calmer.

Held close to Knox, I was reminded of last night in the woods. A wave of heat washed over me despite the cooler air outside. Looking toward the deck, I coughed. "Sorry I threw dirt at your face. Are you okay?"

He grunted and shrugged his shoulders. "I've had worse things done to me." I wondered what others had tried but imagined most opponents were eventually conquered by Knox. He was too strong and too formidable to face many serious threats. He continued, "I was a little surprised, but I can't say I blame you; having a stranger approach you in the woods at night is kind of intimidating."

I grinned. "Yeah. Any more of you guys going to come out of the woodwork?"

Knox said, "Not today." But based on his dry tone, I really couldn't tell whether he was serious.

He carefully set me down on the wooden lounge chair. "Thank you for sharing your story, Haley." I was surprised, but he continued before I could open my mouth, "Ask us more questions and we'll tell you as much as we can. But, the more we know, the better chance we have of finding your dad."

For someone who looked so tough, he had been exceedingly gentle. His manner of speaking also varied widely, sometimes seeming gruff and impatient, and then at other times he could be so caring and insightful. Thinking through last night and this morning, I couldn't help but be intrigued by the dichotomy.

Knox headed toward the house but turned when he had reached the door frame. "Did you know where you were headed last night? Did you have a destination in mind?"

I nodded. "Highway 89."

He ran his fingers through his hair, and I was mesmerized by the array of golden strands glinting in the sun. "I figured as much. Did you even have a map?"

I shook my head then tapped the side of my head with my index finger. He shook his head, grinning. Although I barely knew him, I sensed that he was impressed. "Let us know when you want to come in."

Lounging on the deck, I had a nice view of the forest. I inhaled deeply, savoring the fresh, crisp air and the sounds of birds chattering pleasantly as they flitted from branch to branch. Although it was still slightly cool out, the sun was shining, and I was comfortable in my borrowed sweat pants and long-sleeve T-shirt. Occasionally a breeze whispered through the trees making the branches sway and creak, their leaves rustling.

Forcing myself to believe that Dad had to be safe, I debated what to do. Knox, Chase and Ethan hadn't really given me a reason to doubt them so much, and it was obvious to everyone, including me, that I needed their help. And while I still wasn't sure who the guys were working for, they at least seemed to be on my side. Could I trust that they really were?

The Boardwalk

"Monopoly, Uno, or Checkers?" Chase looked at me expectantly, holding up the three classic games. Their loose plastic pawns rattled gently against each other and the box. Surprised by the question, I didn't immediately respond. "Please, Haley," he implored. "I'm so bored, and I love games."

His adorable smile was too much to resist, especially with his dimple. And the idea of passing the afternoon with a game was infinitely more appealing than continuing to stare out the window and worry about my uncertain future. "Monopoly," I finally suggested, smiling back at him.

"Yes! I love Monopoly. I always pick the battleship. What piece do you want?" He started laying out the game pieces on the table.

I laughed at his enthusiasm, considering my choices. "I've always wanted a dog, so I'll go with the Scottish Terrier."

I watched with amusement while Chase set up the game. He chatted about playing Monopoly with his grandmother and Ethan, and he told me how Ethan always tried to fight him for the battleship. It was nice to see this easy-going side of Chase. He said more in those few minutes than he had the rest of the day put together.

As we got into the game, I had to admit that I was having fun with Chase. I'd never had the chance to do normal things like this with anyone other than my dad and Jessica. For probably the millionth time, I wondered what it would have been like to be an ordinary teenager.

"So, Haley." Chase's voice had an inquisitive tone, and I was slightly worried about what he was going to ask me. "What was it like, growing up with your dad as your teacher? Did he give you straight As?"

I laughed quietly. "My dad was a great teacher. And no, he did not give me perfect grades; I earned them." I confidently moved my pawn and collected cash from the bank.

Chase grinned. "Touché."

"When we first moved out here, my dad was home with me all the time. He focused on the basics — reading, writing, math, and science, but he used every opportunity as a chance to learn. Eventually he transitioned to working part-time, and he gave me more input on what I wanted to study.

The older I got, the more independent my studies became. By the time I was thirteen, he went to work all day, and I completed my chores and my lessons on my own. After dinner, we would sit down at the kitchen table and go over what I had learned. He didn't give me grades per se, but he tested me to see how prepared I was. He asked tough questions, so I always tried to anticipate what he would quiz me on. I learned a lot from him."

Chase purchased a property before continuing with his questions. "That sounds like a good way to learn. But what about friends? Sports? School dances?"

I smiled. "I can't say the idea of a school dance ever appealed to me. As far as sports go, I love running. Plus, my dad took me hiking and camping all the time and taught me basic survival skills. And friends." I paused. "Well, I have one really close friend who moved away last year for college, but we still keep in touch."

"You said you already finished your high school curriculum. Are you planning on going to college?"

The question was innocent enough, but it was a difficult one for me to answer. How could I tell him that opportunities like college had never been open to me? I didn't want him to think poorly of my dad, and I wasn't sure that he would understand Dad's overprotectiveness. "I don't know yet. It's something that my dad and I still need to discuss."

Anxious to deflect, I asked, "What about you? Did you decide to work in private security instead of going to college?" Chase looked a little older than me but was definitely still in the typical college student age range. Since he appeared to be employed full-time, I guessed he wasn't in school.

"Actually, I'm a student at the University of California, Santa Cruz. I'm studying computer science." Apparently I was wrong. How did he manage to go to school and go away for work for days at a time?

He told me a little about the campus and his classes, and I couldn't help but feel jealous. Santa Cruz sounded like the ideal place to live and go to school. I could easily imagine myself biking down the boardwalk on a beach cruiser, the cool ocean breeze in my face. I silently laughed at myself. Such a daydream was pointless, too distant from my current lifestyle to be a realistic possibility.

I turned to Chase, finally asking the question that had been running through my mind since I first saw him in the cabin. "You were following me, weren't you? When I ran into you at the library?" Anticipating his answer, I almost forgot to take my turn.

Chase rubbed the back of his neck, looking sheepish. "Yeah, I was." He paused. "We'd actually been keeping an eye on you and your dad for a couple of days. Although our investigation led us to the area, we had to be sure that we tracked down the correct person. We weren't even expecting Brian Taylor to have a daughter."

"Brian Taylor?" The name sounded vaguely familiar, but I couldn't place it. And then the pieces started to fall into place. Kira . . . Taylor. I hadn't even thought about my former last name when I'd discovered my change in identity.

Chase looked at me, surprised. "Your dad's given name is Brian Taylor. You didn't know that?"

I hesitated. Truthfully, it was embarrassing that my past had practically been a blank slate until a few days ago. "No, I actually just found out about the name change, and I didn't think to ask what my dad's name used to be."

I shook my head, stung that Chase had to tell me Dad's real name. *There's so much I still don't know about my parents, my family*. My heart ached with fear and loss. A few days ago I would have given anything for the answers to my past, the keys to my freedom. *Be careful what you wish for*, I thought.

After a couple hours of passing "Go" and buying and losing properties, we finally finished the game. "Good game," Chase said. "Can you do me a favor and not mention to the guys that you beat me," he said, a teasing grin on his face.

I raised one eyebrow. "Really? I didn't peg you as one of those guys who can't deal with losing to a girl." Chase's soft laugh flowed through me, warming me. I couldn't believe how quickly I had become comfortable in his presence. I think it helped that he also seemed just a little shy, making my own awkwardness less obvious.

"Speaking of the guys, I was kind of hoping that I could make dinner tonight. I'll probably need assistance getting around in the kitchen, but I want to do something to thank you all for helping me." I wasn't used to being waited on hand and foot and was ready to contribute something to the group.

Still sitting at the table, the Monopoly pieces scattered around the board, Chase pulled gently at the neck of his T-shirt. "That's nice of you, but it's really not necessary. Besides, if I let you stand on your feet that long, Ethan will kill me."

I frowned, not one to be easily deterred. Glancing around, I noticed a bar stool and pointed it out to Chase. "How about this? I can sit on the bar stool at the counter and you can just put everything on the counter in front of me."

He hesitated, deliberating as he pushed his chair back from the table. Standing up, he shrugged. "I guess that could work; I can even be your sous-chef. And, I'm sure Ethan will be relieved since he's been stuck with most of the cooking since we've been here."

* * *

It was cozy in the cabin, and I felt relaxed and comfortable. September was always one of my favorite months, and not just because of my birthday. I loved the beginning of autumn, when the sun began to set earlier, making the evening air cool and crisp. Just thinking about it had me craving a warm bowl of soup.

Chase gave me a quick inventory of the ingredients available as I ran through my mental catalogue of recipes. While the kitchen wasn't stocked, we had what I needed apart from tortilla chips and cilantro. Chase texted Knox, asking him to pick some up on his way back to the cabin.

Chase was an excellent sous-chef, not that the chicken tortilla soup I was preparing required much assistance. After years of making dinner, cooking had become routine. Although I wouldn't call myself a master chef by any means, I was a decent cook when it came to the basics. This recipe was an old favorite, an easy standby, that I had long since memorized.

While I chopped, sautéed, and stirred, Chase handed me items from the fridge or pantry and talked about his grandmother's cooking. As he told me about her famous meatball recipe, I could feel the love and respect in his voice. He was clearly close to her and a devoted grandson.

I wondered what my own grandparents were like. My dad had been my only family for so long that I had never really given the rest of our family much thought. And whenever I had asked about them, he gave vague or noncommittal answers that made it clear the topic was not up for discussion. Now that I knew the truth about our lifestyle, I wondered what family I had still living after all these years.

When I finally saw my dad again, I would have to ask him. Dad had been my whole world for so long that I had never really considered a life without him. The thought was simply inconceivable. Now, faced with exactly that situation, I was trying to avoid giving it too much thought. I would find Dad; I just needed to put all his lessons into practice.

The sun was at the horizon and dinner was almost ready when the front door opened. Knox entered and dumped a backpack and his leather jacket on the floor by the door. Closing his eyes, he inhaled deeply. His voice boomed through the small space. "Smells good. What's for dinner?"

Without looking up, I responded, "Chicken tortilla soup."

A few minutes later, Ethan opened the door and quickly spotted me. He glared at me, but I caught the twitch of his lip that was forcing down a smirk. "And just what do you think you're doing?" He walked through the living room toward the kitchen, setting his satchel on a chair as he made his way toward us.

Chase and Knox were standing between the living room and the table. When Ethan reached Chase, he squared his shoulders. "I thought I told you not to let her put any weight on her ankle."

Facing the stove, I only had a partial view of the rest of the cabin. While I couldn't see either of their faces, the tone of Ethan's voice was loud and clear. Already warm from cooking and sitting in front of the stove, I felt my temperature rise a few more degrees. Not wanting to get in the middle, I kept my mouth shut and stirred the soup.

Chase shifted on his feet and sighed impatiently. Ethan waved a hand through the air as if dismissing him. In a lowered voice I heard Ethan say, "I guess I can't blame you; I'm sure she's pretty persuasive when she wants to be." I felt myself blushing and hoped they wouldn't notice.

Dinner was mostly uneventful. I was curious where Knox and Ethan had been all day but couldn't think of a good way to subtly bring it up. Knox and Chase mostly talked sports; Ethan complimented my soup and we discussed cooking.

Toward the end of the meal, I was surprised when Ethan brought up my dad. "Haley, I wanted to let you know that I went by your house today, or what's left of it, and didn't see any signs of your dad. I also discreetly asked around in town, but no one has seen him."

He paused. "No one seemed surprised by my questions. In fact, a few people mentioned that I wasn't the first one making these inquiries. I don't want to alarm you, but I think you need to be on your guard; someone may be after you too."

I listened but pushed the idea to the back of my mind for the moment, not really ready to deal with it. This situation was only creating more questions than answers; one in particular had been nagging me all day. "What did you tell your client about me and my dad?"

Absorbed in what Ethan was saying, I didn't realize that Knox and Chase had stopped talking, and I was surprised when Knox responded. "All we told our client was that we found a man who we believed to be Brian Taylor using the alias Stephen Jones. We provided your dad's work address only and didn't mention anything about you."

Knox paused, scratching his tricep then letting his fingers linger, grasping the muscle. "We gave him that information the morning of the fire, so technically it is possible that he is connected to the men who were following your dad after the explosion. But, like I said before, we can't be sure of his involvement. We just don't know enough about what is going on yet."

I exhaled, feeling relieved. Although the timing was suspicious, the information they gave their client, whoever that was, was pretty vague. And their client may not be connected to the criminals at all. There was still the chance that they didn't actively work for the criminals. My heart lifted at the thought.

Flushed

After dinner, Knox pulled out a deck of cards and placed it on the table. "Who wants to play poker?" Ethan and Chase accepted quickly. Realizing I hadn't responded, Knox turned to me. "Haley, you in?"

I shook my head before Chase chimed in. "Come on, Haley. It will be fun."

"I don't know how to play," I said in a quiet voice.

Ethan smirked. "Don't worry, we'll teach you."

I watched, mesmerized, as Knox shuffled the deck of cards with the finesse of a card shark straight from the movies. "I take it you do this a lot?" I asked, curious how he was so skilled at shuffling.

Knox shrugged. "Poker happens to be one of my favorite hobbies. It helps me unwind." I wasn't really surprised by his admission. I'd already witnessed his poker face on more occasions than I could count, today alone.

While Knox shuffled the cards, Ethan explained the rules of Texas Hold 'em. Chase rummaged through the kitchen for something to bet with. He opened and closed the cabinets, shoving his hand in and searching quickly. At one point Chase called out to Ethan, his voice muffled behind the cabinet door. "Ethan, you better hope I find something to bet with or we're going to have to use your secret stash of M&M's."

Ethan continued explaining the rules without admitting or denying the existence of an M&M's stash. A few seconds later, Chase returned to the table with a bag of chocolate Easter egg candies; a previous house guest must have left them behind months ago. When he pried open the plastic bag, it popped loudly from the release of pent up pressure.

Figuring it would be easier to see the game in action, Knox dealt a few rounds for practice. There were a number of rules and rounds of betting, but it didn't seem too difficult. Meanwhile, Chase dumped the candies onto the table, the small metallic eggs rolling over the wood surface like a bunch of marbles. The overhead light hit them, highlighting their bright, colorful wrappers.

Chase started counting the eggs into four even piles, but before he could pass them out, Ethan swiped a few and popped them in his mouth. Chase groaned. "Seriously?"

Shaking his head, Knox said, "Watch him closely. I wouldn't put it past him to steal your chips so he can eat them."

Ethan grinned. "Oh come on; I'm not that bad. Just be glad they aren't Peanut Butter M&M's. Quit stalling and deal."

After placing the small and big blinds, Knox dealt the cards around the table. His movements were swift and professional. With two hole cards each, the flop was dealt, revealing three of the community cards.

There was another round of betting followed by Knox dealing the turn; then another round of betting followed by the river. Finally, the last round of betting was capped off with the showdown. Some rounds went more quickly than others, ending before the showdown could be dealt.

I was mostly silent, watching, determined to pick up the game quickly. The guys occasionally offered me pointers but generally let me figure it out on my own. They were competitive but encouraging. Slowly, I grew more comfortable with the mechanics of the game and began to relax. Although I was enjoying the game, I was most entertained watching the guys.

Gathered around the table, any thoughts of their jobs or the hierarchy within the group melted away. The room felt cozy and the atmosphere was one of friendly camaraderie. They seemed closer than I imagined was typical for co-workers; not that I knew what normal co-workers, or people, were really like. I wondered how much time they actually spent together.

All three seemed well-practiced in the art of poker, yet I was most in awe of Knox. Knox was clearly in his element, completely cool and relaxed. It was obvious that he was the superior player. He never gave anything away, his poker face masking all of his thoughts and reactions.

Chase took the game very seriously, a trait I'd also noticed during Monopoly. His deliberations were often so long that Ethan would start humming the Jeopardy! tune, or Knox would kick him under the table, urging him to get on with it.

Ethan, on the other hand, didn't take any of it too seriously. I could tell that while he was probably just as competitive as the other guys, he was really just playing for the fun of it. Every so often, I saw him snitch another piece of candy and laughed to myself. It was a good thing he won his fair share of hands, or he would have been out of the game several hands ago.

"So, I have a serious question for you guys." I kept my face completely blank while pausing dramatically. Their expressions turned serious, expecting another conversation about my dad or their backgrounds, I was sure. "Which one of you is responsible for the apple-scented body wash in the shower?" I smiled at the end of the question, unable to hide my amusement any longer.

Chase snickered and Knox guffawed, both turning to look at Ethan. He glared at them. "What? I happen to like the smell of fruit. It's not a crime."

I let out an involuntary giggle, and all three guys immediately turned to stare. Ethan commented, his tone mocking, "Well, look at that. Buffy here not only takes down creatures of the night, she also giggles."

My confusion apparent, Ethan sighed. "Please tell me that you've seen *Buffy the Vampire Slayer*. Television series about a beautiful, kick-ass teenage girl who single-handedly takes down vampires and demons?" *Did he just imply that he thinks I'm beautiful?* Forcing myself to focus, I shook my head at his question. He continued, disgusted. "This is a disaster of epic proportions. We seriously need to hook you up with a Netflix subscription."

Knox interrupted, his voice a low growl. "Excuse me; did you really just compare me to vampires and demons?"

Ethan smirked. "If the boot fits . . ."

As their bantering continued, Chase looked over at me and smiled. Clearly he was used to their behavior. And for the second time that day, I felt a prickle of jealousy. I could see myself being friends with these guys, hanging out and playing games, watching movies. But, I also knew it would never happen. It was strange; they were sitting right in front of me, but I already missed them.

One hand was going particularly well, and it was down to Ethan and me for the showdown. I won the hand with a full house and Knox rewarded me with a smile that stretched to his eyes. I felt warmed to the core and smiled in return.

Ethan looked at me, squinting slightly and cocking his head to the side. His tone was serious. "Are you sure you've never played poker before?"

I grinned. "Positive. Although I have watched *The Sting* about a million times."

Knox's eyebrows raised in response. "Wait. You've seen, and like, *The Sting*?"

I scrunched up my nose and forehead. "Um, yeah. Who doesn't like Robert Redford and Paul Newman?"

The three of them sat motionless, staring at me. Knox broke the silence. "I can't wait 'til Jackson hears this. He's always talking about that movie and how Uncle reminds him of Shaw."

I looked from face to face wondering who Jackson and Uncle were. I remembered Knox mentioned he had a younger brother; maybe they had an uncle too? "Knox, is Jackson the younger brother you mentioned?"

They all started laughing, and I felt like the odd one out, wondering if I had missed the punch line. Knox responded. "No, we're not related. But Jax is like a brother to me. And he's a member of our team."

There were more of them? Hopefully they were in Santa Cruz and would stay there. I didn't know if I could handle one more attractive guy in my life.

As the game progressed, it was easier to see when I should bet and when I should fold. Since I had a weak poker face, I focused on my cards and the odds. I enjoyed the game, the strategy and the luck. I liked being with them, feeling like I belonged even if only for the moment.

I had a hard time thinking that any of them wanted to harm me or my Dad. If anything, hadn't they shown over and over that they were trying to help?

A little voice in the back of my head spoke up. *You don't know who their client is. You don't know what their motives are.*

Maybe not, but I knew that they had rescued me from the fire, even if their appearance there wasn't accidental. I knew that they had looked out for me, taken care of my injuries, fed me, and even entertained me. And deep down, I believed that they couldn't be bad.

Knox yawned and stretched his arms behind his head; we had been playing for a while and it was getting late. My eyelids felt heavy; I was drowsy and about ready to call it a night. Chase shifted in his chair, stretching muscles stiff from sitting so long.

I glanced around the table, sizing up the competition. Ethan's chips were dwindling due to consumption, and he decided to "cash in" by eating the remaining ones. Chase and I had held our own and had about the same amount of chips remaining. Knox was clearly in the lead.

The first three cards were dealt. My hand looked promising, but I couldn't tell for sure. After another round of betting, the turn card was dealt and Chase folded.

With a ten of hearts, queen of clubs, six of hearts, and ace of spades on the table, I was trying not to get too excited. I struggled to still my nerves and keep my face straight. It was down to Knox and me, and it was my turn to bet.

Glancing again at my cards, I checked my hand for what felt like the hundredth time. I was holding an eight and nine of hearts. If only the river would reveal a seven of hearts, then I would have a straight flush. As far as I remembered, the only hands that could beat a straight flush were one of a higher sequence of cards or a royal flush.

Heart pounding, I wet my lips. Looking down at my chocolate "chips," I thought, *Maybe now's the time to go all in.*

Hesitant yet excited, I pushed all of my chips toward the pot, their bright metallic surfaces gleaming as the eggs rolled across the table. I saw the guys perk up, even Knox. I grinned, secretly delighting in their reaction. I held my breath as I waited for the last card to be dealt. *Let the chips fall where they may.*

Between Two Worlds

I smashed a pillow to my face, wanting to scream in frustration. While the poker game was winding down, I'd barely been able to keep my eyes open, certain that I would fall asleep as soon as my head hit the pillow. But somehow by the time I got settled in bed, I found myself wide awake.

It must have been only an hour or so later but felt more like an eternity. Once again, I was unable to shut down the scattered thoughts running laps around my mind. I shouldn't have been surprised. The events of the last few days crashed into my life like a tsunami, leaving devastation I never could have imagined.

All things considered, I was thankful to the guys for providing a distraction from the chaos. While I was busy focusing on whether I could trust them, I wasn't thinking about what I'd found out about my past or what I was going to do about my future. Of course, it didn't hurt that the distraction came in the form of three captivating males.

But awake in the stillness of night, I could no longer rely on those distractions. I lay in bed staring at the ceiling and listening to the sounds of the cabin. Through the thin walls, I heard the gentle creaking of the springs of the sofa bed and the occasional groan of the wood floor. Beyond the walls, the chirp of crickets was punctuated every so often by the hoot of an owl. Normally, sounds like these would have soothed me; tonight they just irritated me, reminding me that I was awake.

Moonlight filtered through the open window, casting a spotlight on the foot of the bed. Shifting positions, I got a whiff of the sheets. Closing my eyes, I tried to imagine myself in my bed at home, longing to smell the familiar scents. I pulled the covers up around me, seeking solace that blankets alone couldn't provide. Would anything ever feel like home again? So far from everything I knew, I ached for something familiar.

Unable to relax my body or still my mind, I thrashed in the sheets. The only home I had really ever known was gone. The bookshelf of novels I had read, the guitar I spent so many hours playing, the cups we drank out of, the blankets I snuggled up under. All gone.

It wasn't even that I missed the things so much as the memories associated with them. They came together to create a feeling of home, a sense of belonging and safety. I felt like the rug had been ripped out from under me.

I got a glimpse of trees swaying outside the window and longed for open spaces surrounded by mountains, the sky a blanket of stars. If it wasn't for my injured ankle, I would have snuck outside to see the stars, even if I had to climb a tree to do so. I needed the feeling of normalcy the night sky provided; I needed that connection to my mom as always, but even more so now that my dad and I were separated.

As I lay there, my thoughts flitted through my mind like small birds darting through the trees, quickly moving from one subject to the next without lingering. Agitated, I threw back the covers and jerked onto my side, clumsily twisting my ankle in the process. "Eek!" The loud sound tumbled out of my mouth before I could suppress it. I waited silently, hoping that none of the guys would come to investigate.

Apparently that was too much to ask for, because a minute later, I heard the soft sounds of the door opening and closing. I didn't bother turning around to find out who it was, feigning sleep instead.

I heard the smooth timbre of Ethan's voice as the other side of the bed dipped from his weight. "I know you're awake. Not trying to make another run for it, are you?" His tone was wry, a quality that I had already come to appreciate as distinctly Ethan.

I let out an inelegant snort in response to his question but refrained from saying anything else. I didn't feel like explaining my turbulent thoughts and emotions.

"Do you need anything?" For once, his voice was serious enough that I could tell he was concerned.

"Nothing is really wrong. I just can't sleep." I kept my reply brief, hoping he would get the message and let me get back to wallowing in peace. "You can go back to bed. I'll be fine."

Ethan chuckled. "Considering tonight's bed is the not-so-comfortable chair in the living room, I'm happy to stay here and help."

He was sleeping in the chair? Obviously it should have occurred to me earlier that there was only one pull-out couch and three guys. Now I really felt guilty for hogging the bedroom. "I'm sorry," I started, but Ethan interrupted.

"Hey now, none of that. I was just pointing out that if you want to talk, I'd be more than happy to stay with you for a little while."

Although I should have told him to go, I found myself giving in. The sound of his deep voice was already soothing me. I turned onto my back and glanced at him in the low light. He was facing me with his knee folded on the bed and his other leg settled on the floor. His palm pressed into the mattress, supporting his weight, while the other was draped across his lap. I couldn't make out the expression on his face, seeing only a slight reflection from his glasses.

I fumbled with the covers, pulling them back over my body, mostly in an attempt to stall having to talk to him. It's not that I was uncomfortable talking to Ethan; I just wasn't used to sharing my feelings, especially in such intimate surroundings.

"I think it's finally sinking in that I don't have a home to go back to. I've led such a solitary life for so many years, all I've really known is that house, the land around it, and my dad." The words just seemed to tumble out, exposing too much. "Usually when I'm feeling down or am having trouble sleeping, I sneak outside and stargaze." I sighed, "And now I don't even have that."

He quickly replied, "You will; your ankle will heal, and you won't be stuck in this cabin forever." He continued, his voice warmer than I'd ever heard it. "Haley, I know it's hard to imagine, but your perspective will change over time. Home is not just a house or even a family. Sometimes it's finding a group of friends that will always have your back or even a career that provides new meaning to your life. Your home as you've known it may be gone, but you will find your place."

He quieted, letting his words sink in. "Your love of stargazing . . . tell me about it."

I couldn't explain the feeling, but I suddenly wanted Ethan to understand. "I've always loved searching for the constellations. They remind me of my mom. One of the few memories I have of her was our secret stargazing.

I remember one night she came into my room after I had gone to bed but long before sunrise. My mom kissed me on the forehead, and I was comforted by the scent of her floral perfume. After gently pressing her fingers to my lips to keep me from waking my dad, we snuck away from the house with a telescope. As she pointed out the constellations, she whispered their names; the-myths associated with them were my favorite bedtime stories."

Ethan slowly moved onto the bed and lay down on his side, his head propped on his hand. "Will you share one of those stories with me?"

I replied, "You really want me to?" He nodded, his hand still cupping his cheek.

I pursed my lips. "Hmmm, that's a tough choice. I think the myth associated with the Virgo constellation has always been one of my favorites. Plus, Virgo is easy to spot; it's the second largest constellation after Hydra."

Ethan grinned. "Perfect. Why don't you tell me that one?"

I sighed, debating where to begin. "Well, as you probably know, myths are often based on oral tradition handed down from generation to generation. They mutate over time, sometimes leading to conflicting versions. There are even several different myths associated with the Virgo constellation. That said, I will tell you my favorite version, the version my mom always told me."

I inhaled deeply, drawing breath to tell the tale.

"The Grecians worshipped many gods, loving and fearing them in equal measure. Most gods lived on Mount Olympus, a place of great beauty and good weather. Several gods dwelled elsewhere, presiding over their own domain; Poseidon lived in the sea, and Hades was lord of the Underworld.

The Underworld was not a place you would want to visit; filled with darkness and the dead, it was a place of no return. As lord of the dark Underworld, Hades was feared as a god of terror and death. Not surprisingly, he didn't have many worshippers or temples."

Ethan snickered, and I continued.

"Demeter was the goddess of the earth, responsible for agriculture and crops. The people of Greece prayed to her, asking for fertile lands and abundant harvests. Demeter had a brother named Zeus, god of the sky and lightning, among other things. Together, they had a daughter named Persephone."

I felt my cheeks warm as I wondered what Ethan thought of this unorthodox relationship. Not wanting to draw attention to it, I continued.

"Persephone was full of life and Demeter loved the child more than anything else. Persephone loved to wander the fields and meadows, often picking wildflowers. Over the years, she grew into a beautiful maiden. Hades was struck by her beauty and fell in love at first sight.

"At the time, it was common for fathers to arrange the marriage of their daughter. One day, Hades asked Zeus for Persephone's hand in marriage. Zeus had quite the dilemma. Hades was a good match for Persephone. But, their marriage would separate Demeter and Persephone forever; Demeter as goddess of the earth could not live in the Underworld, and Persephone as queen of the Underworld would be required to remain there.

"Zeus knew that if he refused, Hades, his eldest brother, would be offended. If he consented, Demeter would never forgive him. Choosing his words very carefully, Zeus told Hades that he would neither give nor withhold his consent. Although Hades wished for Zeus's blessing on the marriage, he read between the lines. Seeing the answer as encouragement, he returned to the Underworld determined to have Persephone as his bride."

Ethan rose up slightly, creating space between his head and the hand that had been supporting it. With the other hand, he removed his glasses. He placed them on the nightstand before returning to his side and laying his head on the pillow.

"One day when Persephone was gathering flowers in the fields, she wandered away from her friends without realizing it. She noticed a beautiful narcissus and knelt down to pick it. Struggling to pull it from the ground, she tugged with all her strength. Suddenly, a giant hole opened in the earth and out sprung a chariot driven by Hades, drawn by steeds as black as night. Hades grabbed the frightened girl and whisked her away to the Underworld; Persephone wept and refused to eat or drink anything.

"When Persephone didn't return that afternoon, her friends were worried. No one could tell where Persephone had gone. Demeter was distraught and wandered the earth searching for her. In vain, Demeter asked both gods and mortals what had happened to Persephone.

"Finally, Helios, the all-seeing Sun, told Demeter what happened, and she was struck with grief. She felt sick at the thought of her beautiful, vibrant daughter living in the lifeless world of the dead. Demeter was furious with Zeus, and she left Mount Olympus to live among mortals in disguise."

Tired of craning my neck to the side, I shifted, laying on my side facing Ethan. The room was mostly dark, but I could make out his face. His eyes were focused on me and I saw his lips part.

"In her sadness, the earth suffered and the crops would bear no fruit. There was a year of great famine, and it seemed as if the whole world would wither away. Zeus couldn't let the situation continue, but he was too ashamed to visit Demeter in person.

"To apologize, he sent other gods to her bearing gifts one after the other, but Demeter refused to listen. She swore she would not let the crops grow until she could see her beloved Persephone.

"Finally, having tried everything, Zeus sent a messenger to the kingdom of Hades to return Persephone to her mother. Hades did not want Persephone to go but knew he had no choice. He asked her not to think ill of him and persuaded her to eat four pomegranate seeds before leaving."

Feeling drowsy, I fought off sleep, determined to finish the story.

"Persephone returned to the earth and was embraced by her mother. The whole world was covered with beautiful flowers; the crops bore fruit once again, and the mortals rejoiced.

"But their happiness at being reunited was to be short-lived. Demeter was heartbroken when she discovered that Persephone had eaten the pomegranate seeds. Knowing that anyone who ate the fruit of the Underworld would be doomed to return, Demeter feared Persephone would be taken from her again.

"Rules were rules, and this one could not be broken. As a compromise, it was agreed that Persephone would return to the Underworld to rule at Hades's side for four months of the year, one month for each pomegranate seed she had eaten.

"Persephone continued to share her time between the two worlds, rising from the dead every spring to return to her mother. Flowers would cover the earth and crops would bloom, celebrating their joyous reunion. There she remained through summer and fall. Every year, when Persephone returned to the Underworld, her mother mourned. Winter arrived and the earth turned cold as ice.

"For all Persephone's beauty there was a sorrow to her, creating something both strange and awesome about her. She was shaped by her time in the Underworld, returning to the earth transformed by her experiences."

I was silent, letting the end of the story hang in the air. My eyelids felt heavy and reality was blurring into sleep.

Ethan spoke, his baritone voice almost a whisper. "As Elisabeth Kübler-Ross so eloquently said, 'People are like stained-glass windows. They sparkle and shine when the sun is out . . .'" He paused and gently brushed my hair away from my forehead. As he did so, my eyes closed.

He continued, his fingers gently tracing the curve of my forehead. "'But when the darkness sets in, their true beauty is revealed only if there is a light from within.'" Ever so softly, he tucked the hair behind my ear.

Flip Flop

Waking up to an empty bed shouldn't have been a surprise considering that's all I've ever known. But when I opened my eyes and the only evidence of Ethan's presence was a slight dent in the pillow next to me, I almost felt like something was missing.

I pulled the covers up over my head in an unsuccessful attempt to hide from my own thoughts. I couldn't help it; I felt my lips curve into a smile as I thought of last night. Ethan had been so sweet, so reassuring.

The gentle touch of his fingers lingered on my skin before the harsh reality of the morning slapped me across the face. *What are you doing, Haley? You cannot get attached to these guys.*

Questions raced through my mind. Had Ethan fallen asleep in here? How long did he stay? I pushed back the blanket and lightly ran my hand over the pillow. It did seem a little warm.

Thinking back, I wondered if I had shared too much with Ethan last night. I hoped he appreciated how personal the constellation myth was to me and tried to reassure myself that he did. Behind Ethan's frequent smirks and wicked sense of humor, I recognized a depth lurking beneath the surface.

Nothing had really happened, but I wondered what the other guys would think. Maybe Chase and Knox hadn't even noticed, asleep the entire time. *Who am I kidding? They would have to be unconscious to realize that Ethan wasn't out there*.

I sat up, rubbing my hands over my face before laughing softly at the thought of what Jessica would think of such a predicament. She was a typical boy-crazy teenage girl, and over the years I often found myself living vicariously through her experiences. I could only imagine how she would react to Knox, Ethan, and Chase. I wished I could talk to her about them.

Finally ready to drag myself out of bed, I limped across the room and opened the bedroom door. Just as I took a step forward, the bathroom door opened and Chase stepped out, nearly crashing into me.

I gasped, startled by his sudden appearance and by his nakedness. Unable to stop myself, I glanced down and was relieved to see he was wearing a long, peach towel tucked neatly at his waist. My temperature started rising and not just from the warm, humid air that slowly flooded the hallway from the bathroom.

Chase laughed, "Oops. I didn't mean to almost run you over."

"It's fine," I stammered, "I was just startled." I really did try to avert my eyes from his shirtless body, but it was hopeless. Moisture clung to his glowing skin, the dew highlighting the contours of his muscles. He had powerful shoulders, toned biceps, and noticeable six-pack abs. His golden tan brought out the gold tones of his tousled blond hair. A few drops of water trickled down his chest, and I watched them disappear below his belly button.

Chase stepped back, suddenly looking embarrassed, pink filling his cheeks. "Sorry about this," he said, gesturing to his body. "My clothes are in the dryer, and I didn't expect you to be up yet. I'll just go get them and get dressed."

I stood there silently as he walked away, stunned by what just happened but admiring his form. Although I had obviously seen guys in their boxers or swimsuits on television, this was by far the closest I had come to a shirtless guy in real life.

Heading toward the kitchen, I passed Chase and tried not to stare. When he bent to dig in a backpack, I could see the clearly defined muscles of his abs flexing. He hastily grabbed a few items and returned to the bathroom. Glancing around, I didn't see Ethan or Knox anywhere and assumed they must have already headed out.

I busied myself, debating what to have for breakfast. I quickly opened and closed cabinets, looking but not seeing their contents. Opening the fridge, I stared for several seconds, relishing the cool air on my face. *Get it together, Haley*.

Breakfast was ready by the time Chase reemerged, this time fully clothed, from the bathroom. Although my ankle was feeling significantly better than yesterday, I still had to limp around, and it made carrying anything awkward and slightly precarious. As I turned from the counter, Chase automatically picked up the dish for me and placed it on the table before sitting down.

Trying to remind myself that Chase was likely more embarrassed than I was, I thanked him and joined him at the table. He finally looked at me, a note of bashfulness remaining in his eyes. "Of course."

Wanting to put him at ease, I tried to think of something to talk about while I ate breakfast. "So, what's the plan for today? More board games?" I had fun hanging out with him yesterday and was hoping for a repeat.

"I may be going out later, but I'm sure we could fit in a few games." He paused. "Actually, I have something I wanted to talk to you about." He rubbed the back of his neck, a gesture I was beginning to associate with nervousness on his part.

"Oh yeah? What's that?" My stomach flip flopped, certain that Chase was about to drop a bomb on me.

"The thing is, we have been wrapping up all of our business in the area and need to head back to Santa Cruz soon."

I tried to keep my expression blank, but my heart immediately sank. I knew they weren't going to stay here forever, but with the craziness of the last few days I hadn't really thought about my next move. And now that I was finally getting used to having the guys around, I wasn't sure I could stand the thought of them leaving. *What am I going to do now?*

Chase looked at me earnestly. "Haley, we want you to come with us."

"What?" My shock was evident. "What do you mean? Like move there?"

"Yes. We want to help you, but we can't stay here indefinitely. We will keep looking for your dad, and in the meantime, you will have a safe place to stay. And we can even help you find a job, if you want." He paused, scanning my face for a reaction. "What do you think?"

I had no idea how to respond. What did I think? Part of me was ecstatic that it was even a possibility. But the more realistic part of me thought it was a crazy idea. *I couldn't really leave with them, could I?*

Perhaps sensing my hesitation, Chase spoke again, his voice softer now. "I know you want to find your dad, but what are you going to do if you stay here? Get a hotel room and wait for him to show back up?" Preferring to see this as a rhetorical question, I mulled it over in silence.

Finally, I spoke. "Chase, it's really nice of you guys to offer. But I don't see how it could possibly work. I can't just move hundreds of miles away while I have no idea where my dad is. How would he ever find me?"

Even as I said the words, I knew that they weren't completely honest. Dad had told me that if the situation arose, I should run and not worry about him. And going to Santa Cruz would get me closer to San Francisco where the safe deposit box was located. While I was sure this wasn't quite what he had in mind, there was no way he could have anticipated this situation.

Chase reached across the table, gently placing his hand on top of mine. "I don't want to overwhelm you, but you need us. You already know that we think there might be someone after you as well, and we can protect you." He paused, and I sensed that he was searching for the right words. "Knox, Ethan, and I have looked at this from every angle, and we think this is the best solution. We want you to come with us."

He gently squeezed my hand before rising from the chair. "We will be in and out today. Take some time to think it over."

Woodenly, I got up from the table and made my way to the deck. Chase was right. What was I going to do if I stayed here? Apart from the meager amount of cash in my purse, I was pretty much up a creek without a paddle. I didn't have a place to stay, a driver's license, a car, or a cell phone. *I can't even walk properly*, I thought. Laughing to myself, the situation seemed utterly ridiculous.

Sitting on the deck chair, hours passed like minutes, my thoughts a jumble of uncertainty. My stomach was in knots. There was still a tiny part of me that worried Chase and the others were working for the bad guys, whoever they were. But the bigger part felt almost sure they were looking out for my best interests.

I didn't want to be naive, but all things considered, going with them was the only thing that made sense. Dad had always told me to run and take care of myself. At the moment, I didn't have the resources to make it on my own. And although I had been suppressing any worry about my personal safety, it was a definite consideration.

* * *

Before I knew it, the door slid open and Ethan popped his head out. "Hey there." My heart did a little flip, and I grinned at him in response. He smiled, his mouth still closed, before opening it to speak. "Want some lunch?"

I shrugged. He said, "Don't go anywhere," before his head disappeared. A few minutes later, he reappeared carrying sandwiches. He handed me one before spreading out on the chair next to me.

As excited as I was to see Ethan, I was concerned that things would be awkward between us after last night. But I shouldn't have worried; he talked to me like nothing had happened, asking about my ankle and making small talk.

Polishing off his sandwich, Ethan breathed a sigh of content. He sipped his drink then spoke. "I stopped by a few more places today to ask about your dad. Still no luck."

Trying to reassure myself that Dad was fine and just staying off the radar, I twirled my hair and stared at the trees. All arrows seemed to be pointing toward Santa Cruz.

Ethan sighed. "Haley, I don't know what's going on here, but I really think you should come with us." Having pretty much already reached that conclusion myself, I felt some of my tension ease. But I wasn't ready to tell them yet. Some small part of me clung to the ridiculous hope that Dad would magically appear.

Ethan got up and offered me a hand. "Do you want to come in for a while?" I grasped his hand, and he pulled me up before looking me over. "Hey, isn't that my shirt?"

I glanced down and nodded. After showering earlier, I was happy to put back on my bra, panties, and shorts, but I had to grab the first clean shirt I could find. The patterned button-down was clearly

Ethan's, and since it stopped about mid-thigh, I rolled the sleeves to my elbows and tied it at my waist.

"It looks much better on you than it ever did on me." I blushed, trying to hide a smile. I felt giddy at the unexpected compliment.

A short time later, Ethan went outside to make a few calls. I relaxed on the couch for a few minutes but started feeling too antsy to sit idly in the silence. Remembering I'd left a book in the bedroom, I went in there to read.

I sat on the bed but quickly realized I could hear the faint sound of Ethan's voice from outside the window. Lulled by the cadence and rhythm of his voice, it took me a minute to realize he was talking in Spanish. I was surprised by how fluent he was.

Inching over to the window, I hid in the shadows, curious about why he switched languages. Ethan was now directly outside the bedroom, and I was able to clearly make out his words.

At first, his side of the conversation sounded pretty mundane, like he was providing an update on what he'd done today. But, then I heard something that froze the blood in my veins. I covered my mouth in disbelief. Replaying the words in my head, I translated them again to make sure I hadn't made a mistake.

"Yes, I think Chase has convinced her to come with us." He fell silent, then, "No, she can't know about that. She wouldn't agree if we told her." More silence. "I know, but we need to get her to Santa Cruz first."

Ethan's words became unintelligible as he resumed walking. While I only heard one end of the conversation, it was clear that they were talking about me. *What can't I know about?* He said I wouldn't agree to go to Santa Cruz if I knew.

Worried that Ethan would come inside and figure out I was eavesdropping, I shut the bedroom door and climbed under the covers. Suddenly exhausted, I figured a nap would be the easiest way to get alone time. Ethan checked on me about ten minutes later, and I told him that I needed to rest after not sleeping well last night.

The certainty I was feeling just a few minutes before slipped away. I had felt so confident that the guys were on my side, Ethan's statements totally threw me for a loop. Even if they sounded worse out of context than they were, I was now doubting my decision. I didn't think I could agree to leave with them when they were blatantly keeping important information from me. It stung to realize that my growing trust in them was misplaced.

I could have confronted Ethan, but the cautious side of me didn't want the guys to know I was suspicious of them once again. It seemed like I would be better off if I just parted ways with them now before things became even more tangled and confusing. Once they dropped me off in the nearest town, maybe I'd have more luck finding Dad on my own.

After a short nap, I emerged from the bedroom and found Knox in the kitchen. "Hi," I said, "I didn't know you were here."

He grabbed a drink from the fridge before walking to the living room and sinking into the armchair. "I just got back a few minutes ago. Sit down for a minute, please," he said, pointing to the chair across from him. My stomach lurched, and I felt like a little kid again, waiting for a scolding from my dad.

Once I was seated, he continued. "I know that Chase and Ethan talked to you about coming to Santa Cruz. I don't want to rush you, but we need to leave by tomorrow morning. Are you coming with us?" The way he said it was casual, almost as if he was asking if I needed anything from the store.

Not wanting to drag this out longer than necessary, I took a deep breath and lifted my head. "I appreciate the offer, but I can't go with you. I need to find my dad, and I should stay in the area."

He sipped his drink then spoke again. "We've been pretty thorough in our search. He may be good at hiding, but if he was still in the area, I think we would have found him by now."

I grimaced, unsure whether I should be grateful or upset that the guys had not been able to find my dad. I opened my mouth as if to speak then closed it again. Finally I spoke. "If you were in my shoes and it was your brother out there, would you leave?"

Knox leaned forward, his green eyes drilling into mine. "I understand where you're coming from, but I think you're making the wrong choice. Your dad is most likely far away from here, probably trying to keep you safe. He wouldn't want you to stay here by yourself, putting yourself in danger."

My hands started to sweat, as I was sure he could tell something was wrong. I hoped my voice sounded more sure than I felt. "Thank you again, but I've made my decision."

Knox relaxed against the couch cushions. "Okay, I'm not going to twist your arm," he said with a small grin. "I think dinner is about ready. Let me help you to the table?"

That was it? I felt a small twinge of disappointment that Knox had given in so easily.

Dinner was a quiet affair. The guys discussed general plans for getting the cabin and cars ready to leave. No one asked me about my decision to stay or what my plans were once they left.

After dinner, I didn't have the energy for poker. Glancing at the clock, I was surprised to find it wasn't that late. I spread out on the couch with a book while they played at the table. The game was more subdued tonight; there was less banter, less animation.

Time seemed to slow. I felt a wave of sadness hit me, realizing that I would probably never see them again. I glanced slowly from face to face, lingering on each. All three were captivating and yet so different from each other.

Knox was such a dichotomy: powerful yet gentle. His striking green eyes could see right through me, allowing no room for questioning or hiding from the truth. Ethan was a mystery. Brown eyes sparkled behind his glasses, a smirk playing at the corner of his lips. Outwardly calm and comforting, there was more to Ethan than met the eye. And Chase, his clear blue eyes honest and true. He was a sweetheart.

My chest tightened. I felt like I belonged with them, and yet I knew I didn't. Ethan's phone conversation had removed any lingering doubts. They would go back to their normal lives and forget all about me in a few days. But I knew I could never forget them.

Even though I'd taken a short nap earlier, I was sleepy and my body felt drained of energy. I read a few words, but then my eyes closed and I drifted to sleep.

Polar Opposites

I opened my eyes, clamped them shut, then opened them again. No change. The sight that greeted me couldn't have been further from the cozy cabin with its low ceilings, distressed wood floors, and views of the forest. I craned my head around wildly, trying to make sure I wasn't imagining things. There was no doubt about it; I had never been anywhere like this.

Judging by the dim gray light that washed over the room, I guessed it was early morning. I was sprawled out on a queen-sized bed with a dark iron headboard and footboard. The larger horizontal frame had curved edges; its thin vertical pieces created the effect of wide jail bars. My limbs were tangled in light gray sheets and a patterned blanket.

I was hit with a massive headache and an overwhelming sense of déjà vu. *Why does this keep happening to me?* For the second time in less than a week, I woke up in a new bed and a completely new place.

I moved my arms and legs, twisting and pulling, struggling to free myself. The sheets felt fresh, almost crisp even. I inhaled, searching for familiar scents. Nothing.

To my right was a large window with a white shade pulled down, letting in enough light to view the room in its entirety. I glanced around the room for clues. Large and well-furnished, each item contributed to the overall effect without cluttering the space. There were nightstands on both sides of the bed, each unique but somehow a pair. A leather arm chair was angled in a corner next to a vintage travel trunk with books stacked on top.

A plane flew overhead, drawing my eyes up the white walls to the incredibly tall ceilings. I noticed that the wall behind my head was covered in warm red brick, reminiscent of an old fire station. Framed photographs hung above me, but they seemed to be mostly landscapes. There was a large door on the wall in front of me. *Where am I?*

I racked my brain. Why couldn't I remember anything from last night? Scanning the room, I saw my bag hanging on a hook near the closet. I wished my dad was responsible for this sudden relocation, but I seriously doubted it.

I bolted upright before realizing I had moved too quickly. My head felt heavy and the room was spinning. The last thing I remembered was watching Ethan, Knox, and Chase playing poker in the cabin. The fog was lifting, and realization was slowly dawning on me. The answer came slowly, turning like an old key in a lock. *Did they kidnap me?*

I limped over to the window and pulled up the shade. My mouth hung open at the sight. The view was of industrial-looking buildings, and I could see palm trees in the distance. If I wasn't so angry with my newest predicament, I probably would have appreciated seeing something that was so completely different from what I was used to. *Are you kidding me?*

I wanted to stomp toward the door, but with my ankle still on the mend, I was forced to hobble instead. My frustration and anger grew with each step, and I grabbed my bag off the chair, but it caught on something. Focused on reaching the door, I yanked at it impatiently without looking. When it didn't immediately give, I pulled harder. Finally, it was released and I stumbled forward. The books on the trunk crashed to the ground, and I swore as their impact echoed off the walls and floor.

The door swung open, and Knox stood in the door frame, ready to spring into action. When he saw me struggling to regain my balance, he relaxed slightly before shooting me a concerned look. "You okay?" He rubbed at his eyes.

Startled by his sudden appearance and full of pent up rage, I clenched my hands into fists at my side and raised my head defiantly. "Knox! What the hell is going on? Where am I? Did you kidnap me?" I was so furious, the words came spewing from my mouth before I could stop them. I angrily crossed my arms over my chest, waiting for a reply.

Knox slowly entered the room, his bare feet lightly padding against the wood floor. His jeans were rumpled, and in his shirtless state, I could see deep creases leading from his hips toward his beltline. I sucked in a quick breath at the sight of his muscular torso and the tattoo that snaked up his bicep and over his shoulder. His hair was disheveled; a lock of dirty blond hair fell over his forehead, partially covering one eye. *Did he just wake up?*

"I wouldn't call it a kidnapping, exactly. More like an involuntary transfer of your person to an alternate location for the benefit of your personal safety and welfare." His lips rose in a crooked grin, enraging me further.

I huffed. "You're joking, right? And don't think you can distract me with your clever response. Where. Am. I?" I seriously couldn't believe this was happening. When the guys gave me a choice to go with them, it never occurred to me that they would end up taking me by force.

"You're at my loft in Santa Cruz." There was no apology in his gaze or tone.

"Well that's just great. And how did I get here?" I thought back to my unexpected drowsiness last night and considered my blinding headache this morning. "Did you drug me?" I knew my voice sounded excessively outraged, but I couldn't believe they would do that to me.

Knox remained stoic, seemingly unconcerned with my accusation. "Haley, I know you're upset right now, but you really need to calm down. We did what we had to do."

Well, that might as well have been a confession. I threw my hands up in the air. "What you had to do? So you *had* to drug me and kidnap me right after I told you that I didn't want to leave? You said that you understood!" I didn't recognize the girl who was yelling right then. It was so unlike me to even raise my voice.

Knox ran a hand through his hair, pushing the stray strands away from his face. "Look. I really am sorry that we had to take such drastic measures. But, it was for your own good."

Knox reached in his back pocket and retrieved his phone. Looking at the screen, he scowled. "I have to go. We'll talk about this later." He started walking out the door before I could even respond. "By the way, we picked up a pair of crutches for you," he said, pointing to the corner. "See you later." I stood there open-mouthed, his loud footsteps echoing as he walked down the hall.

I blew out a quick breath. Holding my hands in front me, I realized they were shaking. I fell back on the bed and sighed loudly. As much as I wanted to throw a temper tantrum and demand answers, I knew it wouldn't accomplish anything. I needed to go into this situation with a level head.

* * *

I heard the sounds of music playing and someone moving around in the kitchen. Did Knox return? I was tired of hiding out in my room, and my curiosity finally got the better of me. Hearing no sounds immediately outside the door, I stuck my head out and surveyed the options.

The door to my room was centered down a hallway; to one direction was a closed door with opaque glass panels, to the other was an opening that led to a large, light-filled room. The music seemed to be coming from the latter. I recognized the song playing as rock from the 60s or 70s, but I wasn't sure of the band.

I grabbed the crutches and crept down the hallway past several closed doors. The music was getting louder, as were the noises coming from what I assumed was the kitchen. I could feel my heart beating in my chest. *Maybe it's Ethan or Chase?* Inch by inch, I moved along the hall, holding my breath the entire time.

Quieting my steps, I peeked around the corner. The hallway emptied into a large, multi-storied room. Based on the size and materials, I realized it must have been an old warehouse that someone converted into a loft. I didn't have much time to dwell on the furnishings or layout because suddenly, a man walked by.

I covered my mouth. *That is definitely not Ethan or Chase*, I thought. He looked a couple years older than me and was pushing six feet tall. His russet colored hair was cut short on the sides but long on top and swooped to one side in a kind of glamorous retro style.

I placed my hand against the wall to steady myself. The wall was cool and solid beneath my palm. At this point I was too far in; all I could do was remain still and try to avoid being seen.

Apparently I had been successful so far because the guy continued about his business. He walked toward an enormous wooden table; surrounded by eight chairs, I wasn't sure it would fit in any other room but this one. He set a glass on the table before drumming on it with his index finger, keeping time with the music.

As he sauntered across the room toward the bookshelves, the song changed and he started dancing, clearly enjoying the song. His body moved with the rhythm of the music, and I was a little envious of his dance moves. He seemed like the kind of person that could just let go and have fun, not worrying about how he looked.

He circulated around the room as he danced, occasionally picking an item up off a shelf or the floor before continuing. His attitude was infectious, and I couldn't help but laugh quietly as I observed him. I was so amused watching him, I almost wanted to start dancing myself.

Playing an imaginary set of drums, he really got into the music. Coming out of his drum solo to resume dancing, he knocked a record off the shelf and muttered, "frack." I covered my mouth to stifle a giggle. After a rather impressive spin, he stopped suddenly. He shuffled back a few steps and did a double-take. When I realized he was staring at me, my heart started pounding.

Surprised, we both stood looking at each other. I cringed and wanted to look away, but I couldn't. He tilted his head and smiled tentatively, the smile quickly building into a large grin.

"Well, what do we have here? You don't have to hide in the shadows." His voice was playful, almost like he expected me but was surprised by me all at the same time.

In spite of myself, I hopped the rest of the way around the corner on my crutches. Hesitant about meeting another new person, I edged into the room, unable to resist his friendliness and the warmth of his gaze. He walked toward me, and his eyes widened slightly as he got closer to me. His smile was captivating. "You must be Haley."

I nodded, nervously running my fingers through my hair before glancing down at my mismatched outfit. *Ugh, I look like a complete mess. Again.*

He spread his arm out as if to take in a vast landscape. "Welcome to our home. I'm Theo, Knox's younger, but smarter, funnier, and better-looking brother." He flashed a mischievous grin, and it was obvious that, if nothing else, he was definitely the funnier brother.

Theo gestured toward a large leather sofa, inviting me to sit. Wanting to distract him from the fact that I'd been spying on him, I said, "I like this song. Who is singing?"

He walked over to built-in shelves holding what must have been hundreds of records and books. He turned the volume down on the record player and then returned, holding an album cover out in front of him. "You are listening to the *Green River* album by the incomparable Creedence Clearwater Revival. Take a good look, because you are going to get intimately acquainted with this album while you're staying here."

Theo's teasing mannerism put me at ease almost instantly. The music continued to play softly in the background, adding to the inviting atmosphere. I laughed and said, "Good to know." I glanced at the vintage turntable sitting in the corner. "I've never actually listened to a record before."

He feigned shock. "What? Now that is just a crime." He wiggled his finger back and forth. "You haven't experienced a song until you've heard it on vinyl. That's pretty much all we listen to around here, so you better get used to it." As Theo was speaking, I noticed a sprinkling of freckles over his face and down his arms. I got a glimpse of a tattoo on his forearm but couldn't see the full design.

He returned the album cover to the shelf, and I was able to take a good look at all of him for the first time. His body was lean but lightly muscled. He wore a vintage-looking T-shirt tucked into light-wash jeans that were rolled at the hem and funny brown and gray wing-tipped sneakers. His whole look was very retro but with a fresh and modern twist. I had never seen anyone that dressed like him, and I immediately liked how his style fit with his fun personality.

I glanced around, admiring the large bookshelves that stretched almost to the ceiling. When I saw the metal ladder to access even more books, I smiled, delighted by my surroundings. Theo must have noticed because he said, "You like it?"

I nodded. "Very much so. I love books and these shelves are awesome."

He grinned. "Thanks! Knox and I designed them."

I couldn't help it, my mouth popped open. "Really?"

"Yeah. We searched for years for the perfect warehouse to turn into a loft. A few years ago, we bought this one and renovated it with the help of Ethan and some of the other guys." He paused, reaching in his pocket. "Speaking of, someone's calling me."

He quickly peered at the screen before answering it. "Hey, Chase. What's up?" After a few moments he looked over at me and smiled. "Sure, she's right here." He leaned across the coffee table and held the phone out to me. "Chase wants to talk to you."

I looked at the phone and hesitated. I wasn't used to speaking on the phone much, and I didn't really know how to respond to Chase right then. I was relieved that he was maybe checking on me but also still upset about the kidnapping.

I finally took the phone from Theo and held it up to my ear. "Hello?"

"Hi, Haley. How are you feeling?" His voice sounded uncertain, like he was worried I was mad at him.

"Other than a headache, I'm okay." I didn't know what else to say, so I waited for Chase to speak again.

"I'm sorry; I'm sure Theo has something to help with your headache." He paused, then, "I hope you're not too upset with us. We really do want to keep you safe and didn't know what else to do."

Distracted by Theo, much of my earlier anger had dissipated, at least for the moment. And Chase's voice sounded so sincere, it was difficult to stay angry with him. For some reason I didn't hold Chase as responsible as Ethan and Knox. If anything, Chase seemed like the one who would have disagreed with the plan or want more time to deliberate. But, I also didn't want to immediately roll over and act like everything was okay.

"I can't say I'm thrilled that you guys decided to take matters into your own hands."

Chase's voice softened. "I understand, but I have to admit that I'm glad you're here. It sounds like you already met Theo; he's going to hang out with you today, show you around. He's a really nice guy, and I think you'll like him." When I didn't respond, he continued, "Are you okay with that?"

Not seeing another choice at the moment, I said, "It's fine."

"Great! I know you usually don't get out much, so hopefully you'll have fun."

Chase and I ended the conversation, and I hung up the phone. I handed it back to Theo, our hands gently brushing during the transfer. Theo popped up from his chair, clasping his hands in front of his chest. "I'm being a terrible host. Would you like a drink or perhaps something to eat?"

He paused, and I felt like he was assessing my appearance. "Maybe a shower?" He scrunched his face. "What are you wearing?" He said it in such a way that I couldn't help but laugh.

My cheeks felt hot, and I looked at the couch. "I don't know how much Knox told you about me, but these are the only clothes I have."

He grinned, mischief dancing in his eyes, and then spoke in a mock-stern voice. "Well that is completely unacceptable, and we need to go shopping. But first, you should probably shower; you can borrow some of my clothes in the meantime." He walked toward the stairs.

I smiled despite my reservations about the proposed shopping trip. I wondered what shopping with Theo would be like. If nothing else, it had to be more entertaining than shopping with my dad at the few department stores in Carson City.

These guys were quickly taking over my life. But if I had to be honest, it was hard to be too upset with them considering I was finally getting one of my long-standing wishes fulfilled. I was in a new place with endless opportunities.

Classic

Exiting the loft on my crutches, I stopped momentarily as Theo locked the door behind us. While I wasn't particularly looking forward to the shopping aspect of this trip, I was definitely excited to explore somewhere new. And I had to admit that I was in desperate need of clothes. Fortunately, Theo had loaned me his vintage red Coca-Cola T-shirt. It was still loose on me, but I didn't feel like I was swimming in it like I was in Chase's or Ethan's clothes.

I scanned the vehicles parked along the curb, wondering which one belonged to Theo. There was a mix of cars, trucks, and SUVs, some older and some newer, but none seemed quite right for him. I heard a car beep before Theo said, "It's just beyond that truck."

I didn't know much about cars, but I could tell this one was a classic. With its candy-apple red color, chrome accents, and sleek design, I'd never seen a car that was so manly and pretty all at the same time. "Wow. What kind of car is this?" I didn't dare touch it as we approached, certain it must have been worth a small fortune.

"This, my dear, is a 1967 Mustang. She's a beauty, isn't she?" He said with a grin. He opened the passenger door and waved his hand, inviting me to get in.

My mouth opened in shock. "We're taking this to go shopping?"

He shrugged. "Why not? It's technically Knox's car, but he's nice enough to let me take it out for a spin now and then. Come on, hop in. It's shopping time." He was practically jumping up and down with excitement, and I laughed at his enthusiasm.

"This is Knox's car? For some reason, I pictured him riding a motorcycle."

Theo scoffed. "Oh, he does. I'm sure you'll see the black beast soon enough. But Knox basically lives and breathes cars, so he has several. The Mustang is his baby since he spent years restoring it to pristine condition."

I couldn't help but be impressed. Clearly there was more to Knox than muscles and a gruff personality.

The seat squished pleasantly beneath me, warming my legs. The leather smelled fresh and the interior was immaculate. Theo closed the door with a flourish before practically skipping around to the driver's side.

Theo smiled as he drove with one hand on the wheel, the other leaning against the window sill. It was a nice day, and we had the windows cracked letting the fresh air breeze through. I glanced from side to side, trying to see as much as I could without gawking. As we drove away from the loft, the area became more residential and then changed slowly to a row of shops.

The main street had a mix of one- and two-story buildings that looked older but had fresh paint. The large glass window storefronts, flowers outside, and colorful window displays created a charming effect. Some of the shops were stationery stores, others had flowers in the window, and many had clothing or household items. With parking spots lining the street in front of the stores, pedestrians traversed the sidewalk and street.

When Theo pulled into a parking spot near the upscale-looking boutiques, I looked around nervously. "Um, do you think we could go to Kohl's or Target instead? I don't have much money." I had stuffed my only cash in my pocket before leaving the loft, and I guessed that it wouldn't go far in this neighborhood.

"Don't worry about it. This shopping trip is on Knox, so you might as well take advantage of it. I may even have to buy myself something pretty," he said with a cheeky grin.

I hesitated. I felt a little better with Knox paying, but my stomach still clenched with unease. "I don't know."

Without responding, Theo jogged around to my side and opened the door. "Haley, get out of the car. I promise not to go overboard . . . at least today." He grabbed my crutches from the back seat and held them out, waiting.

Reluctantly, I slid off of the leather seat and took the crutches. "Okay, let's go." Maybe we could just pick up a few things quickly and be on our way. Somehow, I doubted that.

It was still early in the day and despite the sunshine, chilly under the shade of the store awnings. Fortunately, there weren't many other people out; navigating the sidewalk on crutches with shop doors opening and closing was enough of an obstacle course. Theo strode along beside me, confident and focused. I tried to imagine Knox being this excited about shopping and almost snorted aloud.

We passed a few clothing stores but moved on after I shook my head; one had western-style outfits and another was full of short skirts and crazy patterns. So far, nothing really looked like anything I would wear. Finally, Theo opened the door of a shop, smiling and inviting me to enter as a small bell rang in the distance, heralding our arrival.

Stepping over the threshold, I was surprised by how inviting the store was; it felt almost cozy.

Music played softly in the background, muffling the sounds of the few other shoppers. A subtle floral scent drifted through the air.

Clothes hung around the edges with large wooden tables scattered throughout. The tables displayed a variety of items: jeans, T-shirts, folded sweaters, even jewelry. There were several well-dressed mannequins. Distracted by my observations, I hadn't even noticed that Theo was no longer standing with me until he popped up at my side holding a dress.

I looked at it and scrunched up my nose. It was an orange-red color and had a short hem and cutout back.

Theo sighed. "Okay, Haley. You're going to have to help me out here since you haven't liked any of my suggestions so far. What is your usual style?"

I looked at him in confusion. It was a question that had never crossed my mind. My dad wasn't any help with clothes, so I had always just chosen inexpensive pieces that fit comfortably. It had never occurred to me to consider my style, or if I even had one.

"I honestly don't know. I don't have any experience with fashion." I glanced around the store, hoping something would catch my eye. Spotting a tailored chambray shirt, I held it up. "How about this?"

Theo tilted his head, looking at the shirt and then scanning me from head to toe. "So, you're a classic girl. Okay, I can work with that. You should pair that top," pointing to the chambray shirt, "with these capris," grabbing a pair of coral capris in a light denim fabric. "Size six, right?"

Surprised, I nodded. "How did you know?"

He grinned as he led me toward the fitting room, selecting a few other items along the way. "Good guess."

Seeing what Theo indicated was the fitting room made me pause. I was used to the standard hallway of white doors where you picked one and it was basic but had a lock. How could he expect me to go behind a velvet curtain strung across a rod like a shower curtain and take my clothes off? *Someone could walk in at any moment!*

I swallowed and stepped into the small space complete with a full-length mirror and stool. If Theo said it was okay, and obviously other shoppers had to do the same, I figured I was overreacting. Theo hung the clothes on a rod and then held me lightly by the shoulders. "You have to show me everything you try on, even if you don't like it, so I can get a better feel for fit and style. Okay?" I nodded, distracted by the adorable freckles that kissed the bridge of his pale nose and cheeks.

As I slipped on the first outfit, I wondered at my lack of embarrassment when Theo looked me over and then guessed my size. Apparently I felt comfortable with him in a way that was a complete surprise. I knew if I'd had the same encounter with

Ethan or even Chase, my face would have turned an unflattering shade of red.

When I stepped out of the fitting room, Theo immediately walked toward me, eyeing me closely. "Turn around," he said, twirling his finger.

I slowly turned in a circle and then watched him, curious for his reaction. For once he wasn't smiling; instead, his expression was all-business. After a few long seconds of silence, he finally spoke. "That top isn't right. It's too trendy. And the jeans are okay, but we can do better. Next outfit."

After modeling everything Theo picked out, we settled on the chambray shirt, coral capris, and a pair of jeans. Theo ripped the tags off the shirt and capris and told me to change while he went to pay. I felt strange putting on clothes we were buying right then, but I was relieved to look more presentable for the rest of our shopping trip.

As I approached the counter, I noticed that the sales girl was leaning on the counter talking to Theo. She was probably a few years older than me and very pretty, with shoulder length black hair cut in a sleek bob. Her makeup was dramatic; her eyes were lined in black and her lipstick was deep red, giving her the look of a modern day Snow White.

Theo laughed at something she said, and I hesitated, almost feeling like I was interrupting. She saw me then and straightened, handing the shopping bags to Theo.

Theo must have noticed the change in her demeanor and followed her gaze. Spotting me, he winked. "There's my partner in crime." The girl looked she'd just taken a bite out of a poisoned apple.

I followed Theo out the door. Now that he had pinned me as a "classic girl," he no longer pointed out store windows seeking my response. Theo carried the bags as we walked down the sidewalk with a sense of purpose.

I probably shouldn't have brought it up, but my curiosity got the best of me. "So, do you know that girl?"

Theo stopped in his tracks, "What?"

"The girl in the last shop. I thought maybe you knew her since the two of you seemed friendly."

Theo started walking again. "Oh, no, I don't know her. She was just being nice because it's part of her job. Anyway, did you know that the word 'jeans' came from the French word for 'Genoa' because Genoase sailors wore clothes made from denim material?" As he continued spouting random fashion facts, he seemed to be talking faster and faster. *Is he nervous?*

The day had warmed up and there were more shoppers out; wearing my new clothes, I almost felt like I fit in. Passing small cafés with outdoor tables and flower boxes, the smell of coffee and savory food drifted by. I looked at the diners' faces and studied them as they laughed, talked, and ate. *Is this what normal people live like? Is that what I look like, even if just for the day?*

Theo slowed as we approached another storefront, breaking me from my reverie. When he cleared his throat and shifted from one foot to the other, I looked closer at the shop, confused. Once I saw the frilly garments on display, understanding dawned. *This should be interesting.*

"So, I thought you might want to do this shopping without me. But, I can go in with you if you need my help." His eyes widened, and then he stuttered, "Not that you would need my help, help. I just meant, I can stay with you if you don't want to be alone." I would have found his flustered rambling endearing if the situation hadn't been so awkward. Apparently my easy comfort with him only went so far.

Thankful that he was giving me a choice, I quickly replied, "No, I'll be fine."

His shoulders dropped in relief. Pointing to a coffee shop directly across the street, he said, "I'll be over there getting a much-needed caffeine fix. Do you want anything?" I shook my head. "Okay, I'll be watching for you, so just wait right here when you're done." He quickly shoved a few bills in my hand before he opened the door to the shop and waved good-bye.

Entering the store, I felt like I was stepping into another world. The space was small, intimate, and suffused with the smell of fresh flowers. The lighting was dimmed, and sheer white curtains filtered the bright sunlight from outside.

A crystal chandelier hung over a circular table topped with a rainbow of lace panties fanned in a circle. Beautiful antique mirrors with glass-etched patterns added to the illusion of being inside a jewel box. Carved tables and gilded armoires showcased an astounding array of bras and various other undergarments.

With a name like "Underwear" there was little doubt in my mind as to the goods sold. But some of the items astounded me: plastic bras that adhered to your chest like giant stickers, lacy dresses, and items that didn't seem to cover much at all. Fortunately, I found underwear, bras, and casual sleepwear that were more my style. While I cringed at the cost, I dreaded Theo's response if I returned empty-handed. I breezed through the dressing room and checked out quickly, anxious to be done.

When I stepped outside, I held my hand up to shield my eyes from the glaring sun. Almost immediately, Theo exited the coffee shop and jogged across the street. "Apparently we need to pick you up sunglasses too. But let's take a break first and get lunch."

We dropped the shopping bags off at the car before stopping at a charming café for lunch. After a delicious salad and a break from my crutches, I felt refreshed.

When we approached another clothing store, Theo opened the door for me. "This store should be a little more to your taste. I bet we can finish most of our shopping in here."

Energized by the possibility of finishing soon, I put more effort into looking for clothes that I liked.

As we wandered around, Theo asked, "So, Haley, what's your favorite color?"

"Sapphire blue," I responded instantaneously.

He peered down at my right hand. "I'm not surprised, considering your ring. And it's your birthstone, right?"

How did he know when my birthday was? *Oh yeah, Knox or one of the others must have mentioned it.* "Yes. The ring was actually my mom's." I bit my tongue. Why did I tell him that?

"It's a beautiful ring." He must have sensed that I was feeling uncomfortable because he continued on and changed the subject while he gathered more clothes for me to try on.

This was one of the few stores we had shopped in that also had men's clothing, and apparently Theo couldn't resist the allure. He fingered collared shirts in a variety of colors and patterns, and I could hear him muttering excitedly to himself. Stopping at a plaid one, I heard the name "Ethan" as he nodded to himself. *Does he shop for Ethan too?*

When I entered the fitting room this time, the bar was full of clothes to try on, mostly selected by Theo. I noticed several pieces in blue and smiled. Apparently he approved of my favorite color.

I made quick work of the pile, finding many options that I loved. Since Theo had already established my general style and size, pretty much everything he picked out worked. But when I got to the last dress on the bar, I groaned. It was gorgeous, but I would never pick it out for myself. I was tempted to put it with my other discarded items but doubted Theo would let me get away without at least showing it to him.

As I slipped it on, I relished the feel of the silky fabric against my skin. The dress was a beautiful sapphire color and fit me like a glove. My bra peeked out from the thin spaghetti straps, but I didn't dare try the dress on without it. The neckline dipped into a deep V, showing just enough cleavage to draw attention without exposing too much. It was fitted down to my waist and then flared at my hips. The short hem was somewhat extended by a few alternating stripes of white and sheer fabric, each about an inch in width.

I smoothed my hands over the fabric and sighed. I was slightly uncomfortable with how revealing the dress was. But I also knew that I had never looked better. It actually reminded me of the dress I'd worn on my birthday but was much nicer and definitely more flirtatious.

I stood fidgeting and looking in the mirror, still wondering if I could avoid showing Theo. I sucked in a few deep breaths. *Come on, Haley. Just do it.* I pushed back the curtain and took a small step out of the fitting room. I expected Theo to walk toward me like usual, but he appeared to be frozen to his chair. He blinked rapidly before continuing to stare, his focus unwavering.

"Sweet Sassafras."

He twirled his finger once again before resting it momentarily on his lips; I obediently turned in a slow circle. As he approached, I hesitantly asked, "It's too much, right?" I had no idea what he was thinking, but I was certainly feeling self-conscious.

Theo looked stunned. "Too much? Are you kidding me? You are absolute perfection in that dress."

I nervously twisted a strand of hair around my finger. "Are you sure? Don't you think it's, um, a little too tight? And too short?" I glanced down my body, still a little surprised to see so much uncovered skin.

Theo gently pushed up my chin with his finger and said, "Haley, look at me." I forced myself to stare into his eyes and for the first time noticed that they were an intriguing shade of hazel instead of brown like I'd originally thought. With dark green around the edges and a coppery brown toward the pupil, I stood transfixed.

"The fit is divine. I promise." He gently turned me until I was facing the mirror. Pointing to my shoulders, he continued, "See how these delicate straps show off your lovely collar bone and décolletage?"

I blushed and looked away, but he pressed on. Lifting the fabric away from my stomach, he said, "See how the fabric lays against your skin but doesn't cling?" He lightly placed his hands on my hips and my skin burned at his touch. "The seam here even falls right at your natural waist, showcasing your hourglass figure."

He paused for a moment, skimming his eyes down to the hem. "And, this dress is in no way too short. Why not show off your legs?" His grin widened as he likely noticed the rapidly spreading pink staining my cheeks.

I stared into the mirror, astonished by Theo's appreciative comments. I considered myself pretty in a normal girl sort of way, but his reaction to seeing me in this dress made me feel extraordinary.

Theo stepped back and leaned against the wall outside the fitting room, letting out a breath. "Haley, this dress is obviously outside of your comfort zone, but I really hope you'll get it. The fit and color are perfect for you, and I think you'll end up regretting it if you don't."

Unsure what to say, I slowly nodded, "I'll think about it." I shut the curtain and carefully removed and hung up the dress. I sat down on the bench and slumped against the wall. *Who knew trying on a dress could be so . . .* I searched for the right word *. . . intense?*

Despite my initial hesitation, I had truly enjoyed the day with Theo. He intrigued me. He clearly had a vast wealth of knowledge and yet, he seemed very creative, artsy, sensual even. Although I had just met Theo this morning, I already felt like we had been friends for years.

Sneaking Suspicions

I stood in front of the guest room closet, debating my options. Since I didn't know what I would be doing today, I finally selected pink shorts and a lightweight navy and white striped sweater. After slipping on my new pair of gray canvas sneakers, I considered my reflection in the full-length mirror and smiled. For the first time since my birthday, I looked like my usual self, although somewhat improved due to the nicer clothes. I had to give Theo credit; he knew how to pick out clothes that were both flattering and comfortable.

I should have felt guiltier about letting Theo spend Knox's money to buy me clothes. But Knox's hand in my kidnapping helped assuage some of that guilt. I knew it probably wasn't rational to blame him for the decision to drug me and bring me to Santa Cruz, but I didn't care. Although the guys had never stated that Knox was in charge, his authority at the cabin was obvious. His unapologetic attitude when I confronted him yesterday still made me grind my teeth in frustration.

As annoyed as I was with Knox, I felt the most betrayed by Ethan. After opening up to him and sharing memories of my mom and the constellation story, I could have sworn we had a connection. While he genuinely seemed to care about me, the phone conversation I overheard shattered that illusion. And, technically, if I couldn't trust Ethan, that meant I couldn't trust any of them.

After just a week around these guys, I felt like I was riding on a perpetual roller coaster. One minute they were sweet and thoughtful, the next they were controlling and acting shifty. I knew I was perhaps overly suspicious thanks to my dad's influence, but I couldn't ignore all of the signs that things didn't totally add up with these guys.

Part of me screamed to run away as fast as I could. But another part knew my best chance of finding out more information about their intentions and my dad's disappearance was to stick around. And, as much as I hated to admit it, I was relieved that they hadn't left me alone in the woods with no money and nowhere to go. I hadn't been able to justify making the decision to go with them, but now that I was here, I planned to take advantage of it.

Deciding that I'd spent enough time lost in my thoughts, I grabbed my crutches and headed toward the living room. Theo was there, putting his laptop in a beat-up brown leather messenger bag.

He looked up and gave me a welcoming smile. "Good morning, cutie. Love the outfit," he said with a wink. "I'm actually heading to the library to work on a group project. I left bagels on the counter, or help yourself to anything in the fridge."

I sat down on the sofa and watched him get the rest of his stuff together. "Okay, thanks." *He's leaving me alone? And did he just call me "cutie"?*

He walked toward the door, pulling his bag over one shoulder. "Make yourself comfortable, and I'll see you later."

Sitting on the leather sofa, I remained the picture of calm relaxation, but my insides danced with anticipation. As soon as the door shut behind Theo, I jumped up. *I'm alone. Alone in the loft.* I had been itching to explore, to see what the rest of the space was like and to find out more about Theo and Knox. Now I had my chance.

Although I had already seen the kitchen, living, and dining room, I used this time to take a closer look. Admiring the work and design that had gone into their home, I couldn't possibly imagine them anywhere else. Thanks to the light-filled interiors and wood floors, the space felt airy. And yet, the large furniture in heavy materials and the metal accents on the railing and fixtures kept it grounded.

Despite its industrial framework and overt masculinity, their home was still inviting and homey. I supposed it was thanks to all the details throughout, definitely Theo's doing.

Walking toward the immense bookshelves, I tried to gauge their size. With such high ceilings, everything had to be oversized to not be overwhelmed by the sheer scale of the building. Not only were they tall, the shelves spanned two walls forming a large L-shape.

I marveled at the number of books; it almost looked like they had raided a library. Running my fingers along their spines, I scanned the titles. Some looked newer than others, and they seemed to be organized topically. The books ranged in subjects from woodworking and criminal psychology to fashion and art history. There was even a large fiction section, complete with many of the classics.

Even with all the books, the shelves had more than enough space for other items. There was a nice balance of decorative items and books, creating an overall effect that was pleasing to the eye. Their extensive record and movie collection took up several shelves. I hadn't even noticed the TV, large as it was, distracted by all the books. *Who needs TV when you have all these books?*

I scanned the rest of the living room and stopped when I reached a giant trunk on wheels. Reminded of the old movies I loved to watch, I laughed. *Maybe they're magicians too? They certainly did a good job of making me disappear*. I was curious about the trunk but had more important things to explore, like Knox's room and the rooms upstairs.

I turned and headed toward the dining room. The living room, dining room, and kitchen were combined in one large area, but there were still clearly defined rooms. The areas were designated by the furniture yet flowed seamlessly from one to the next.

I skimmed my fingers along the rectangular table top, admiring the beautiful wood grain. Stopping, I leaned forward, unable to detect any seams and very few knots. I couldn't imagine how large the tree would have to be to get a single piece this large.

The sun streaming in the kitchen windows blinded me momentarily. Apart from a large island that ran parallel to the dining table, most of the cabinets and appliances were placed in an L-shape, mirroring the bookshelves. Unlike my kitchen in Coleville, this kitchen had no upper cabinets, leaving the space nice and open.

The dark gray cabinets contrasted nicely with the wood floor and the light stone countertops. Despite the ample counter space, the countertops were mostly bare. I took a mental inventory: a fancy looking coffee maker, a knife block, and a container holding cooking utensils.

Walking along the length of the table, I eyed the second floor. I set my crutches against the wall; then with one hand on the metal rail, I hesitated at the foot of the stairs. *How much time do I have before someone returns?* If I went upstairs, I couldn't just sprint back down to the living room and pretend I hadn't been wandering around. Curiosity got the better of me, and I shrugged. *If I get caught, I'll come up with something.*

I held onto the rail, using it as a crutch to help avoid putting too much weight on my ankle. It was cold and hard beneath my hand. Climbing the stairs, I reassured myself I was making the right choice. I felt entitled to some snooping; after all, they had kidnapped me.

The wood floor and metal stair railing continued up the stairs and onto the second floor. I reached the second floor landing and turned right to continue down the walkway. I noticed that thick wood beams ran in parallel lines across the second-floor ceiling.

To my right was the metal railing overlooking the kitchen, dining room, and living room; to my left was a concrete wall with several doors. *Behind door number one*, I thought. I knew the first door belonged to Theo's room, although I had yet to see it. The door was partially open and I peeked my head in. With no one in sight, I listened for any sounds of movement.

I entered the room tentatively. I felt slightly guilty entering Theo's personal space without being invited since Theo had been so kind and welcoming to me.

The wall in front of me was red brick, like the one in the room I was staying in downstairs. Apart from the placement of the door, and what I assumed was an extended closet, the size was much the same. But, the ceiling was different; the parallel wood beams continued into the bedrooms.

Although the style of the room matched the rest of the loft, it definitely had its own flair. It even had its own scent. I sniffed, trying to put my finger on it. The smell was inviting, calming even. I closed my eyes, inhaling deeply. There were notes of citrus, lavender, and perhaps rosemary. Combined, the flavors created a scent that was at once clean, refreshing, and relaxing. I smiled. *The perfect complement to Theo.*

The headboard backed up to the wall with the windows, the bed facing the closet. Two nightstands flanked the bed, each with a lamp. The one to the right of the bed held a tidy stack of books and a square leather tray with various items in it: loose change, a pair of sunglasses. I scanned the titles, wondering what Theo found interesting: *Washington: A Life*, by Ron Chernow; *Willpower*, by Roy F. Baumeister and John Teirney; and *The Count of Monte Cristo*, by Alexandre Dumas. *I'd like to read all of those!*

The brick wall had framed pictures on it, much like the ones in my room. While those downstairs were mostly landscapes, these were a mix of cities, famous landmarks, and other travel-related scenes. Many of the photographs had the same feel to them, and I wondered if maybe Theo or Knox had taken them.

A few feet away from the foot of the bed a long and narrow wooden desk spanned much of the wall. The desk chair was wooden with wheels and looked like it belonged in someone's office long ago. There were few items on the desktop and any papers were sorted into trays and folders. The top paper in the tray appeared to be some of Theo's homework. I was impressed by the bright red "A" before I even realized he was listed as "Theodore Bennett." I smiled; the name had a nice ring to it.

A large calendar hung on the wall above the desk next to a bulletin board. I leaned forward to get a closer look. There was a picture of two children I assumed were Knox and Theo, magazine clippings of bikes and men's fashion, a cocktail recipe, and some random quotes.

Opening the door to the right of the desk, a light immediately flickered on. I stood speechless, admiring the lines of clothing hung in neat rows on matching hangers. Long and narrow, the closet stretched the length of the room. Toward the end, a set of shelves several feet wide went from floor to ceiling. Pairs of shoes were lined up on display. *What guy owns this many shoes? This many clothes for that matter?*

I closed the door gently and returned to the upstairs walkway. I peeked my head in the next door. Realizing it was a bathroom, I didn't linger. The next door was open, revealing another bedroom.

Does someone else live with Theo and Knox? If not, why do two guys need four bedrooms?

The room was decorated much like the bedroom downstairs with several noticeable differences. The ceiling of this room had wood beams, the windows were larger and arched, and there was slightly more space. I wondered why Theo chose the room he had. Given the choice, this was the room I would have picked.

I quickly surveyed the furnishings but sensed it was another guest bedroom. The closet was empty of clothing, confirming my suspicions. Still anxious that someone was going to return to the loft, I hurried out of the room.

Arriving downstairs, I felt calmer, although I still felt like I was being watched. *Don't be ridiculous, Haley.* I grabbed my crutches and then turned left, heading down the hallway toward my bedroom. I breathed a small sigh of relief. At least they would expect to find me down here.

I knew that a bathroom and guest bedroom lay behind the doors to my left. What I really wanted to know was what hid behind the door on the right and the one at the end of the hall. Assuming Knox didn't have an opaque glass door for his bedroom door, I figured the one on the right side of the hall must lead to his room.

I stared at the door, wishing I could see through it. I didn't want to imagine how Knox would react if he found me snooping around his room. *Wait, why am I even hesitating?* I straightened and took a deep breath. Grabbing the handle, I swung the door open defiantly. I quickly glanced around and released my breath when I saw that the large room was empty of anyone else.

In front of me was a window as wide as the bed centered beneath it. I tilted my head to one side, eyebrow raised. With no bed frame, the mattress rested directly on a large rug placed on the wood floor.

I stepped onto the rug, feeling its soft fibers respond beneath my feet. The bed was inviting, covered in plush layers of sheets and blankets in varying materials and shades of gray and white. If the bed had been a person, I would have said it was in a state of undress. It didn't look sloppy, it just looked relaxed; I wanted to fall into it.

On each side of the bed, a dark metallic lamp was attached to the wall, pointing toward the pillows. There were no nightstands, but I figured the bed was so close to the ground you could just set books or items on the rug.

Knox's room had two interior doors; I discovered that one led to a bathroom, the other to a closet. I stuck my head in the closet, turning on the light. His clothes hung neatly and the floor was clean. Although the space was smaller than Theo's closet, it still felt somewhat spartan in comparison. I gently flipped through the hanging items. *Knox owns a suit?* I had only ever seen him wear jeans and T-shirts.

The rest of the room was much like the closet; there were few items beyond the essentials. On the brick wall to the left of the bed was a simple wooden desk, no drawers or shelves. A laptop, notepad, and a cup of pens sat on top. I flipped through the notepad; it was mostly mechanical drawings of gears or rough sketches of rooms with dimensions. *Private security, huh?*

I heard a car door shut and my heart lurched. I turned my head and eyed the door to the room feeling momentary panic. *Is someone coming?* Feeling jumpy, and not wanting to press my luck any further, I returned to the kitchen. There were dishes from breakfast that needed to be washed anyway.

Standing at the sink, my back was to the rest of the loft as I looked out a window. My hands were covered in soapy water, the smell of the lemon-scented soap clean and pleasant. I washed the dishes, mesmerized by the bubbles and the repetitive motion.

When I heard the front door open, I figured it must be Theo or Knox returning. I finished washing the remaining dish, rinsed off my hands, and dried them on the kitchen towel. I turned, expecting to see a familiar face; instead, I practically jumped out of my skin.

Hartfelt Apologies

I yelped in surprise at the sight of the tall
stranger standing in front of me. I probably should
have been worried that he was an intruder, but I was
too busy speculating whether he just stepped off the
pages of a Ralph Lauren ad. With his sun-kissed skin,
pale blue polo, and white shorts, I could easily
envision him on the deck of a sailboat, staring off
into the distance.

His shirt was just snug enough to display the
outline of his muscular chest and biceps. His glossy
raven-colored hair was curly but cut short enough to
lay in perfect waves. Dark brows hovered over
piercing blue eyes that seemed to bore into me with
intelligence and purpose. His chiseled face was
softened only by stubble that simultaneously looked
rough and groomed.

When he spoke, his tone was formal but
friendly. "I apologize for startling you, Haley. My
name is Jackson Hart." *Jackson? This must be the guy
Knox mentioned the other night.* He held out his arm,
initiating a handshake. I hesitantly placed my hand

in his, hoping that he didn't feel my tremor at his touch.

I stepped back, trying to get a handle on my nerves. "Is there something I can help you with?"

His stance was casual, but somehow his demeanor betrayed an overall sense of authority. "Yes. I need to speak with you about a few things." Gesturing to the dining table, he said, "Would you mind taking a seat?"

Too intimidated to even consider arguing, I sat in the chair he indicated. I twisted my hands in my lap, uncertain why Jackson wanted to talk to me.

After sliding into the seat diagonal from mine, he got right down to business. "First of all, I would like you to know that my team has fully briefed me on the circumstances of the past week." *His* team? While I had assumed Knox was in charge based on my previous observations, obviously I was wrong. Amazingly, I could imagine Knox following orders given by Jackson. While Knox was the epitome of raw strength, Jackson personified calm and control.

"On behalf of the entire team, I would like to apologize for the method that was employed to bring you to Santa Cruz. I hope you know that it was done with your best interests in mind."

Taken aback by his impromptu apology, I remained quiet, weighing his words. I couldn't help but wonder how they could possibly know what was best for me when, at that moment, I had no clue.

Seemingly unperturbed by my silence, he continued. "It is my understanding that Knox and Theo have offered to let you stay here at the loft for the time being. Is that acceptable to you?"

It hadn't occurred to me that I had a choice in the matter. But, even without asking about other options, I knew I wanted to stay at the loft. I felt comfortable here, and it just seemed like the right fit. Plus, after spending the day with Theo yesterday, I was looking forward to more time with him. Somehow I could imagine us becoming really great friends.

"As long as it's not too much of an inconvenience, yes, I would like to stay here for now."

Jackson's deep blue eyes drilled into mine, searching. I wondered what he was thinking but didn't dare ask. "Good." He scrolled through his phone, as if consulting a list, and then continued.

"Next, I want to emphasize that you need to stay with one of the guys on the team at all times. They have been instructed to follow a rotation system based on their availability. Obviously since Knox and Theo live here, they'll be around more than the other guys."

At this news, I gasped in dismay. "I don't need a babysitter! I've been here by myself all morning, and I'm fine." I couldn't believe the gall of him to demand that I remain with one of the guys all the time. Maybe I was a prisoner here after all.

As I was stewing over Jackson's news, another thought hit me. "Wait, are you saying that Theo is a part of the team? He's in security?" Considering Theo's engaging personality, it never even occurred to me that he had the same job as Knox and the others.

Jackson leaned back in his chair and draped one arm along the top of the chair next to him. His relaxed posture seemed at odds with the serious topic of conversation. "Yes, Theo works part time since he's still in school. And actually, Knox has been in the garage the whole time, so you haven't been alone. The loft has a sophisticated security system, so he would know if you attempted to leave." *Oh crap. Did that mean they had security cameras around the loft? What if Knox caught me snooping?*

Unaware of my internal dilemma, Jackson proceeded. "And while I can appreciate your position, I must insist. Our constant presence is for the benefit of your safety, I assure you."

As difficult as it was to argue with him, I spoke up. "I don't understand. Why is my safety an issue here in Santa Cruz?" It didn't make sense. The guys had supposedly taken me away from the Coleville area for my safety. No one else should even know I was here.

"Yesterday, we discovered that two men visited the home of your neighbor, Mrs. Martinez, asking questions." *Jessica's mom?* Oh, no.

Concerned, I interrupted. "Is she okay? They didn't hurt her, did they?"

For the first time, Jackson's voice warmed, losing its cool, professional tone. "She is perfectly fine. There is no reason to believe that she is in physical danger. But, we are concerned that she may have provided the men with information about you. So, you need to be extra cautious while we are still investigating this situation."

As much as I despised the thought of the guys being forced to babysit me, his reasoning was sound. I was sure Mrs. Martinez would never intentionally hurt me, but she may not have realized why the men were asking questions. And it was probably too much to hope that the men had been unable to understand anything she said due to the language barrier.

Giving in seemed to have become my default these days. But, knowing I didn't have room to argue, I consented. "Okay, I will stay with the guys as directed. But don't think I'm happy about it." I gave him a small smile, hoping he would realize that I was joking . . . sort of.

Jackson's lips lifted slightly in response, and I relaxed a little. "Thank you, Haley. Finally, I wanted to let you know that I have found a potential part-time job for you at our office. The official title is a temporary office assistant, but you will basically be doing administrative work. Does that sound like something you would be interested in?"

My heart raced in excitement, but I didn't want to get ahead of myself. "I don't have any work experience, but I would be happy to do administrative work. Also, I don't actually have a formal high school diploma or identification, and I would prefer to stay off the radar as much as possible. Is that going to be a problem?"

He didn't appear at all disturbed by my admissions. "Don't worry about any of that. Based on what the guys have shared about you, I'm sure you will have no trouble with the tasks required for the job. And, since it is a temporary position, it will be simple to keep you off the books."

For not the first time, I found myself curious about the private security company. *Why are they so willing to give me a job when I don't even have proper identification? That's not normal, right?* I started picturing a dinky office in a strip mall with stained carpet and the smell of burnt coffee permeating the air.

Jackson stood up, clearly ready to leave now that his business was complete. "I will move forward with getting things set up. The office is in San Jose, and you will be riding to and from work with one of the guys. Since your position is part-time, we will work your schedule around the team's availability."

He gave me a polite smile, "Haley, it was a pleasure meeting you. I'm sure I'll be seeing you again soon." And with that, he walked out the door.

I remained at the table, stunned by what had just transpired. It didn't help that Jackson Hart was so good-looking. As attractive as my other new acquaintances were, Jackson was in a completely different league. He had tall, dark, and mysterious down to an art. And at this point, I couldn't tell if I was intrigued or disconcerted.

* * *

Considering I was going to be staying here a little longer, in Knox's home, I figured it was time to clear the air. *How could he be here and I didn't know it?* I thought through the layout of the loft and wondered where he was hiding. I hadn't yet been behind the opaque glass door on the first floor hallway; maybe the answer lay behind it.

I got up from the table and grabbed my crutches. Once I reached the end of the hallway, I hesitated. Was I supposed to go in there? I knocked, but when I received no response, I gingerly opened the door. I peeked my head around, unsure what I was going to find.

A wooden table with metal legs and metal chairs sat in front of a garage door made of glass overlooking a delightful patio and garden. The glass door was a design feature I'd never seen before but immediately loved; it was an industrial loft's equivalent of extravagant French doors. The garden was small and intimate, surrounded by the brick walls of other buildings.

I entered the room, noticing the potted plants on the stained concrete floor. A large chalkboard hung on the brick wall to my left, covered in stunning chalk art. To the right was a spiral staircase made of iron. My eyes followed the staircase to the second floor where about thirty or forty glass jars covering exposed lightbulbs hung from the ceiling. Imagining them lit at night, I smiled; they would probably look like giant fireflies.

I debated whether to head upstairs or outside, but the matter was settled when I heard noises coming from my left. Previously distracted by my new surroundings, I had failed to notice a door to the left of the chalkboard. Although the door was thick, I could make out a radio playing, scarcely covering the sounds of metal occasionally clanging on concrete. Considering Theo's comment yesterday about Knox and cars, it seemed likely Knox was behind the door working in a garage.

I knocked on the door but wasn't surprised at the lack of a response. With some effort, I pushed the door open as it squeaked on its hinges. The radio and sounds of the garage grew louder, and the smell of damp concrete, motor oil, and metal mingled in the cooler air.

The space was large with several bays, some with cars; dark metal tool boxes lined almost an entire wall. Glancing around, I didn't immediately see Knox, so I continued walking. With no windows, the space was lit by fluorescent lights and the natural light streaming in through several large skylights. Peg boards hung above the tool boxes, covered in meticulously organized tools of all shapes and sizes. I was amazed by the number of items one could need for working on cars.

Finally, I spotted a pair of jeans with leather boots attached to them sticking out from beneath a car. Now faced with the prospect of actually talking with Knox, I wanted to turn and run. Before I could, Knox rolled out from under the car and spotted me. *Crap*.

I froze, unsure what to do. Since I was the one intruding, it seemed like I should be the one to speak. "Sorry. I knocked, but there was no answer, and I guessed you were in here since I could hear noises."

He stood up and grabbed a white towel stained with black streaks. His muscles flexed as he wiped his hands on it, and I noticed smudges across his forearms and face. His skin glistened from exertion, and his dark T-shirt clung gently to his chest. It was a good look on him.

"Did you need something?" His voice was gruff as usual.

I looked down at the floor. "I met Jackson. It sounds like I'm going to be staying at the loft a little longer, which I assume you already knew. I was hoping we could talk more about why you felt the need to kidnap me."

He sighed, stuffing a hand in his pocket. "Look, Haley. My hands were tied, and I wasn't going to waste time dealing with your stubbornness. I knew you needed to get out of there." He spoke in an even tone.

I gripped my crutches. "That's it? So did you have anything to go on other than a hunch that I wasn't safe?" Unlike our earlier confrontation, my voice was more controlled this time.

He scratched his chin with his free hand. "At first, no. But on our last night at the cabin, there was a break in at your dad's office. His file was taken."

I frowned. "Why couldn't you have just told me that?"

"Because even if I had told you, I wasn't sure you would agree to come with us. And I didn't want to take that risk."

Knox brushed his hair back from his face, his green eyes staring into my own. I could easily picture him giving Theo a similar look, and suddenly everything clicked. He was trying to protect me.

I may not know why he cared, but I knew that he did. Whether he and the other guys were responsible for everything that had happened or not, he had gone above and beyond to make things right.

I remained silent, considering, and then nodded slowly. "I still wish you had talked to me, but I am very grateful for all you have done." I paused. "Thank you for letting me stay here and for the new clothes."

"Don't mention it. You're welcome to stay as long as you want." His face was unreadable as ever, but beneath the stony exterior, I sensed that this was his way of apologizing.

Ready for a change of subject, I cleared my throat. "So, where are the bats?"

Knox raised his eyebrows and tilted his head. "Huh?"

"You know. The bats." I leaned forward as if to share a secret. "Isn't this your Batcave?" I whispered conspiratorially.

He laughed, the sound deep and hearty, and I smiled in return.

"No bats. But lots of cars, cars that put the Batmobile to shame. Want to take a seat?" He gestured to a stool nearby.

He stood in front of the hood of the truck, and I sat on the stool watching, curious. I didn't want to break his concentration so I stayed silent. While still looking at the hood, he spoke. "Do you know much about cars?"

I laughed. "Not really. Apart from how to drive one and how to change a tire."

He nodded. "Those are both important skills; at one point that was the extent of my knowledge too."

Looking at the hood's contents, hands on hips, he seemed intent on solving something. Seeing him in the garage, I smiled to myself; it felt more like his home than any other part of the loft. While I imagined the process of fixing cars could be frustrating at times, it also seemed like it could be intensely gratifying. Sensing that Knox had worked out his latest kink, I figured I could speak now without interrupting his thoughts.

I fiddled with a loose screw sitting on top of the nearest toolbox. "How did you become so interested in cars?"

He picked up a part. "I guess it was like most things — part necessity, part interest." He grabbed a tool from the floor. "I used to pick up odd jobs when Theo and I were younger. I noticed that I was most interested in the ones that involved cars, and not just because they paid the best. At first, I had no clue what I was doing, but I gained skills and knowledge over time."

I continued playing with the screw, watching Knox while he worked. "My dad and I used to love listening to *Car Talk*. Click and Clack, and many of their callers, were hilarious. Our truck was pretty old but ran well. I kept hoping that something would break just so I could call them. I imagined imitating funny truck noises; then they'd tell me how to fix it, and I would be able to."

Knox looked up at me and grinned widely, his mouth still closed. The smile reached his eyes, and I could feel his approval.

I snickered. "Obviously, that was kind of far-fetched considering the extent of my knowledge."

He chuckled. "Perhaps a little, but it doesn't have to be. You could learn."

I grinned. "I'd like that."

We remained there a while, me sitting on the stool observing, Knox working on the car. We talked occasionally, but silence felt just as natural as talking. Used to seeing Knox in crisis mode, it was nice to see him at home. I liked him better this way; living with him temporarily may not be so bad after all.

I didn't realize how much time had passed until my leg started falling asleep. I stood, gently shaking it. Debating whether to ask my question, my insides danced with anticipation. "So, will you show me black beauty?"

He sputtered. "Black Beauty? That's a horse. I think you mean the black beast," his voice sort of growling playfully at the end.

I laughed. "Yeah, that's the one."

"Sure, I'll even take you for a ride sometime."

Admissions

I re-read the same sentence for the third time before shutting the book with a sigh. Knowing that Ethan could show up at the loft any minute was making me ridiculously antsy. I glanced at the clock again, the hands moving agonizingly slow toward eight o'clock. Even though it had been five days since overhearing his phone conversation, the sting of his duplicity was still fresh. I just wanted to get this over with so I could move on with the day.

Trying to distract myself, I watched Theo completing his homework at the dining table. It was odd seeing him in serious mode since he was usually so lighthearted. Of course, his clothes still gave off a fun-loving vibe. Today's vintage tee was mostly covered by a casual tweed blazer, the sleeves pushed up to his elbows. His dark-wash jeans were once again rolled at the hem, displaying a pair of well-worn Converse sneakers. The combination probably would have looked odd on most guys but somehow looked effortlessly fashionable on Theo.

I was glad he volunteered to be my personal shopper and style guru. Now that I was starting a new life, however brief, I felt more motivated than usual to make an effort. And since I was visiting campus with Theo and Chase today, I even put a little extra time into diffusing my long, wavy hair and picking out the right outfit. *Now, if I can just get rid of these stupid crutches . . .*

As if on cue, I heard the front door open, and Ethan strolled in. My heart started pounding, a mixture of nerves and anticipation. He was the picture of confidence, dressed in dark slacks and, of course, a patterned button-down shirt.

I stood up to greet him and his eyes took me in from head-to-toe. "You look nice. But, I sort of miss seeing you dressed in my clothes," he said with his trademark smirk.

Already embarrassed, I felt even more awkward when Theo came over and casually slung his arm around my shoulder. "Doesn't she look great? And you haven't even seen the good dress yet," he said with a suggestive wiggle of his eyebrows.

I avoided Ethan's gaze, unsure how he would react to Theo's easy display of affection. "Is that so? I'm looking forward to it." He took a step toward us, "Now, it's time to look at that ankle. You've been using your crutches, right?" I nodded.

I took a seat on the couch, and Ethan sat down close enough that our knees were almost touching. He drew my leg up and rested it on his thigh while he examined my ankle. "Any pain when you put full weight on that foot?"

"Not for the last day or so. It feels much better." I refused to look at him, hoping he wouldn't realize how uncomfortable I was feeling around him.

He lightly ran his thumb over my ankle a few times, and I automatically looked up at him in surprise. From behind his glasses, his warm brown eyes searched mine, silently inquiring. *Can he tell that I'm trying to avoid him?*

"Well, as long as you're not in pain, you can go without the crutches. But, I don't want you to overdo it, which means no running yet."

I moved my leg away from his. "Okay, thanks. It will be a relief just to walk normally again."

Ethan looked at me for a long moment before standing. "It was nice to see you kids, but I'm late for work. See you later?" He was looking directly at me, so I nodded before saying good-bye.

After he left, I felt my anxiety melt away. Hopefully it would be easier by the next time I saw him. I knew I'd eventually have to confront him, but I wasn't ready for that just yet.

Theo went into the kitchen and came back with a gift bag and a playful grin. "Here's a little gift to celebrate kicking those crutches to the curb."

"What? Theo, you really shouldn't have."

"Oh, shush. Are you trying to spoil my fun?" He pushed out his bottom lip into a small pout. "Please?"

Unable to resist his endearing charm, I laughed. "Fine."

I opened the gift to find an adorable pair of cork sandals with a wedge heel. I slipped them on and buckled the ankle straps. They fit perfectly and were surprisingly comfortable.

I hopped up from the couch, my skirt fluffing gently with the movement. Wearing what felt like a goofy grin, I said, "Thank you, Theo. They're perfect."

He gave me wide smile. "Of course they are." He tugged my hair gently. "Okay, let's hit the road!"

* * *

Today we were riding in Theo's Outback. We bypassed the highway and drove on side roads for maybe ten minutes before we reached the entrance to campus. It was clear that we had arrived when a large redwood sign greeted us: "University of California Santa Cruz."

Driving over rolling hills nestled among the redwoods, we passed signs for various schools and even a campus farm. The roads and sidewalks were bustling with shuttle buses, students on bikes, others walking, and some in cars. As we drove, Theo threw in random bits about the campus and its history. I was amazed that the campus had over twenty-five miles of hiking trails.

We turned off the main road and headed toward a large building. Several stories tall, it was covered in large squares of alternating metal and glass. It reminded me of an enormous rectangular Rubik's Cube. The bike rack was full, and students walked by, passing the sign that said "Engineering."

I finally spotted Chase standing outside the building beneath a group of trees. Wearing khaki cargo shorts and a button-down chambray shirt rolled up to his elbows, Chase looked even better than I remembered. He had on a backpack, and his hands were grasping the straps; when he spotted Theo's car, he smiled and waved. My heart fluttered happily in response.

Theo pulled up to the curb and Chase came around to open my door. I hopped out and saw his eyes widen as he quickly looked me over, making me blush slightly. He reached a strong arm around me for a quick one-armed hug. "Hi, Haley." I smiled and squeezed back automatically, surprised not only by the impromptu hug but how natural it felt.

Theo waved at us from across the passenger seat. "I'm off to class. Catch up with you for lunch. Be good!"

As Theo drove off, I suddenly felt shy, and I sensed that Chase did as well. I busied myself watching the passing students, intrigued by their clothes and hair. Some hurried by, some listened to music, and others talked with fellow students or on their cell phones.

Chase cleared his throat. "I thought you might enjoy a day on campus. Fortunately it looks like you ditched the crutches. Are you up to a little bit of walking? Our campus is pretty spread out."

I grinned and lifted my foot. "We will see about these shoes Theo gave me, but it would be nice to stretch my legs."

Walking in the shade of the redwoods, the sun gently warmed us, but the air was cool and clear. I couldn't imagine a more beautiful campus. As we walked, Chase pointed out various buildings, from exercise facilities to student centers and dorms. Absorbed in the tour, I was startled when we were suddenly engulfed by students that swarmed into the courtyard outside.

Chase shook his head. "Class must have just let out. Stay close."

Surrounded by so many people was unlike anything I had ever experienced; I was immersed in their colors, their smells, their voices. Overwhelmed by the sheer number of people, I felt like a fish swimming upstream against the current. I was thankful to have Chase at my side as we moved through the crowd. His arm briefly brushed against mine, and my skin tingled in response.

Amazed, I spoke, mostly to myself. "So. Many. People."

Despite the chatter of other students, Chase must have heard my remark. He laughed gently and looked toward me before a look of concern clouded his face.

Once we had cleared the path of the other students, he gently touched my back. "You okay?"

Slightly out of breath but grinning, I responded. "Yeah, just not used to seeing many, well any, people, really."

He nodded knowingly, one side of his mouth lifting. "We have a decent number of students on campus, around 17,000." I felt my eyes widen. That was more people than the combined population of Coleville and Minden, plus some.

Past the crush of students, it didn't take me long to relax again and enjoy the scenery. Despite feeling overwhelmed at first, being around other people was a rush. I felt energized by the movement and the sheer newness of the experience.

After a quick tour of the library and a stop by the outdoor pool, it was almost time to meet Theo for lunch. For the second or third time since I had been on campus, a girl smiled at Chase. But when she looked at me, I felt like she was sizing me up. I didn't stop to dwell on it; thanks to all the walking and the excitement, my stomach was growling.

As we neared the café, Chase dug his hands in his pockets. "I'm glad to see you enjoying yourself. I hope now that you're here we'll get to hang out under more normal circumstances."

I rolled my eyes playfully. "Yeah, normal circumstances." I paused and spoke again with a more serious tone. "I would like that. Maybe I can beat you again at Monopoly." I smirked.

Before Chase could respond, Theo showed up. Theo was full of energy despite a full morning of classes. He led us upstairs before stopping to open a glass door with the name "Terra Fresca" etched on it. Theo said it was one of his favorites on campus because it was a little nicer than the dining halls and offered table service.

Regardless of the food, I could see the allure of the café. The inside was cozy with upholstered chairs, small round tables, bookshelves, and even a fireplace. Large windows overlooked the forest and sunshine poured through the trees. Groups of students clustered around tables eating and conversing.

We sat at a round table and quickly ordered before Theo started talking again. "So, Haley. Have your major picked out yet?"

I snorted, the idea of me going to college seemed preposterous. *And yet*, I thought, *here I am*.

Theo pouted. "Come on, at least humor me and tell me what you would pick."

Without hesitating, I replied. "Astronomy."

Theo smiled. "Now that wasn't so hard, was it?"

"Your turn. What's your major?"

Chase laughed as if I had made a joke. Theo glared at him before turning to me. "Mr. Studious thinks it's funny that I've changed my major once or twice because I couldn't narrow down my many interests."

Chase nodded. "'Many' might even be an understatement. In the past few years, you've started rock climbing, tango dancing, and cycling. You originally enrolled as an anthropology major, quickly switched to philosophy, then considered linguistics before finally settling on the history of art and visual culture, whatever that means."

I laughed as Theo elbowed Chase. "Okay, thank you. I think we get the point." He straightened, lifting his chin proudly. "I prefer to see myself as a modern-day Renaissance man."

I sipped my water and set it on the table. "So what exactly is the history of art and . . . whatever Chase said?"

"It's basically traditional art history on steroids. Since images can play a role in perceptions or a reflection of a belief or value, they give us clues as to what is important not only to the society they were created for but also the creator. In other words, we study images from the past and present — whether a painting, video game, or even a tattoo — and consider the social impact."

The waiter finally arrived with our food. We were all so hungry that we dug in and the conversation lapsed momentarily. When I finally slowed down, I saw yet another student in a "Banana Slugs - No Known Predators" T-shirt walk by.

Many students wore graphic tees, but I kept seeing this one in particular, and it stuck out to me. Looking at Theo and Chase, I bit my lip before speaking. "Speaking of images, what's up with those T-shirts?" I inclined my head toward a passing student wearing one. "Don't they know that raccoons eat banana slugs?"

Chase and Theo glanced at each other, scarcely suppressing surprise and amusement. They both started to speak before Chase nodded to Theo to take over. "First, don't hate on banana slugs; they are our revered and feared mascot." I couldn't resist laughing before Theo shot me a playful stink eye.

He paused to pick up some food on his fork and then pointed it at me. "Second, why do you know so much about banana slugs?"

I shrugged. "Growing up, my dad and I went for walks in the forest. We had a deal, a game, really. Whenever I encountered something new, he told me the name only. I could ask any questions I wanted, but he would only answer 'yes' or 'no.' After returning home, I'd usually research the plant, animal, bug, whatever."

Even Theo was silent for a moment, his eyebrow raised. Was my admission that strange? The waiter returned to refill our drinks, and I was thankful for the distraction.

At the unexpected memory of my dad, I felt a pang of guilt. Although I was happy to be here, I hated that it came at such a high cost. I would trade all of my new experiences just to know that my dad was okay. Hit with a sudden wave of sadness, I picked at my food while Chase and Theo talked.

When I heard Chase mention Jackson, my ears perked up. "Speaking of Jackson, have you guys heard when I am going to start work? He spoke to me about the job when I met him a few days ago, but I haven't heard anything since."

Chase shook his head. "No, but he's been kind of busy. He did mention that we should all come to his uncle's house this weekend to hang out. You could talk to him about it then, or I can call him now, if you want."

"No, that's fine. I'll talk to him this weekend." Relieved that I'd have a chance to find out more in a few days, my mind wandered to the many other questions I had about what the guys did and where they worked. There was one that immediately came to mind, and it was out of my mouth before I even realized it. "Jackson kept referring to the 'team'; how many of you are there?"

Between bites, Chase answered, "Six." *Six?* Holding my hand under the table, I counted. *Chase, Ethan, Knox, Theo, Jackson*. Realizing that was only five, I wondered what the sixth member of their team was like.

Theo said, "I forgot you haven't met Liam yet! He's going to love you!"

Interested to learn more, but deciding to move on, I asked, "So, what can you tell me about my new employer? I realized after talking to Jackson that I don't even know the name of the company." I kept my voice even, hoping they wouldn't realize the depth of my curiosity.

Chase and Theo exchanged a subtle look, and I caught a twinge of hesitation on Chase's face.

Theo responded, "Well, that one is easy. The name of the company is Zenith. We work at the San Jose branch, but there are also branches in a few other states. The office is located in a skyscraper downtown."

"Zenith, huh? I like the celestial name." When they both looked slightly confused, I continued, "You know, a zenith, the highest point in the sky?"

Chase nodded, "Oh yeah, I guess I'm so used to hearing the name that I forget its meaning." He paused. "You weren't kidding about choosing astronomy as your major, huh? You seem to really like the subject."

I nodded. "That would be putting it mildly, but yes." I refused to say more, not wanting to admit the extent of my obsession.

Theo clapped his hands together. "This is awesome! Do you know how popular stars and celestial bodies are right now? I am already picturing clothes and jewelry that we can buy for you!"

I smiled and shook my head. We just went on a mini shopping spree and he was already buying me shoes and thinking about what to purchase next.

When the waiter arrived to retrieve our plates, Theo spoke. "I've got lunch; you guys go ahead. I know you have some stuff to work on, Chase."

I reached to pull out my wallet, but Theo immediately objected. "Haley, what do you think you're doing? Put that away before I throw it in the trash." I rolled my eyes at his extreme reaction.

Theo grinned mischievously. "Don't think I wouldn't; you need a new one."

I hunched slightly. "Are you sure I can't pay for my share?"

He glared at me. "Absolutely." He paused, placing a credit card with a giant cartoony banana slug in the leather folio.

As we pushed in our chairs, Theo looked pointedly at Chase. "Don't let her out of your sight. I've seen quite a few guys checking her out. Maybe I shouldn't have let her out of the house in that dress." He winked at me, and I felt heat rising from my chest to my face.

I was quiet on the drive back to the loft. What would Dad think if he could see me now? I thought about all of the things that had changed in the past week: a new city, different clothes, friends, and even a job. Would he see these things as proof that I could live a "normal" life? Was this even normal,

surrounded by five (soon to be six) guys, always
guarded by at least one of them?

Elegant Accents

I knew it was almost time to leave, and I could feel a thin layer of sweat forming on my forehead. Clothes were strewn across the bed, and I had just pulled on a shirt. I fumbled around in the closet, looking for my cork wedges, frustrated by what seemed like a futile search. *I don't even have that many clothes; where can they possibly be?*

Knox's voice called down the hall. "Almost ready, Haley?"

I squeaked, throwing a few more things in the large canvas tote bag and tugging my shirt down to cover my stomach. Knowing that we were going to Jackson's uncle's house to hang out with the other guys, I had debated my outfit several times, wondering if it was dressy enough, too dressy, too fill-in-the-blank. Now that it was time to leave, I wanted to hide in the closet.

Knox's voice was closer now. "Everything okay in there?"

"Be right out." I answered quickly, hoping that would be enough to keep him from coming in to check on me. Normally very tidy, I didn't want him to see the room in this state, or worse yet, catch me between outfits. Finally spying the wedges, I slipped them on before throwing the remaining clothes in the closet and shutting the door.

After locking up the loft, Theo, Knox, and I headed out to the garage. I wondered what car it would it be this time. It seemed like every time I went somewhere lately, I was riding in a different one. I still hadn't been on the black beast. *Yet*, I thought, reminding myself of Knox's promise to take me for a ride.

Knox pointed toward a black truck, and I had a sudden flashback of this truck sitting in the woods outside the cabin in Markleeville. It seemed so long ago, and yet I knew it was just after my birthday. I shook my head. *Whoa, has it really been almost two weeks since my birthday?*

Despite my lack of a consistent schedule, I was easily settling into my new life, especially now that I was free of the crutches. I alternated between hanging out at the loft, running errands, and seeing more of Santa Cruz. Like Jackson had promised, at least one of the guys was always with me, which usually meant some variation of Theo, Knox, and Chase. So far, I had avoided facing Ethan again. Knowing he would likely be there tonight, as well as Liam—who I had yet to meet—made my pulse race.

"Shotgun," Theo yelled, jogging to the truck ahead of me.

Knox growled, "No. Haley gets the front."

I looked back and forth between them, wondering if I should get involved. "Oh, it's fine. I don't mind sitting in the backseat. Theo's taller anyway."

Theo playfully stuck out his tongue at Knox, "See." He put our bags in the back before holding out his hand to help me climb in the tall truck. Its interior was spacious and immaculate, complete with black leather seats, dark tinted windows, and a high-tech dashboard with digital maps and a backup camera.

I mentally counted Knox and Theo's cars, quickly tallying four: the Mustang, the black beast, Theo's Outback, and the truck. *Private security must pay well*, I thought. *Or maybe Theo and Knox came from a family with money?* Somehow that didn't quite seem to fit.

As I was pulling the seatbelt across my stomach, Theo stopped me. "Sit in the middle so I can see you." I moved to the middle seat and caught Knox watching me in the rearview mirror. He rolled his eyes at Theo, and I laughed out loud.

It was fun seeing the brothers like this. Although I had been spending time with each of them at the loft, we were rarely all three together. Knox was mostly absent, and according to Theo, work was crazier than usual for him. I wondered how much of that was related to the situation with my dad. Hopefully busy was a good thing in this instance.

The garage door closed, and a Willie Nelson song started playing through the stereo. Theo groaned and immediately grabbed Knox's cell phone from the cup holder. "You are not going to make us suffer through Willie and Waylon this entire trip." A few seconds later, another song started playing.

Knox snatched his phone from Theo and changed it back to Willie. "You know the rules. My truck, my music."

Interrupting their bickering, I said, "Hold on a second."

Before I could continue, Theo cut me off. "See, Haley doesn't want to listen to that either. Now you have to change it."

"No, that's not it. I'm fine with Willie Nelson." Theo groaned again. "I just wanted to ask how you're playing music through Knox's phone. It isn't plugged in anywhere."

Theo turned around and gave me a surprised look. He reached back and patted me on the cheek, "Oh, our sweet, sheltered little Haley doesn't know about Bluetooth."

Embarrassed, I realized that I should have figured it out. "I've heard of Bluetooth, but I've never used it. I didn't know you could use it to play music as well as talk on the phone."

Knox tucked his phone in his pocket before smacking Theo on the arm. "Stop making Haley feel bad." He gave me a small smile through the rearview mirror. "The technology hasn't been used for that purpose for long. It's not even standard in most cars yet." Knox merged onto highway seventeen northbound.

Theo's face lit up as he turned to look at me. "Speaking of cars, Haley, I have a very important question for you."

"Okay . . ."

"What is your dream car? And make sure you think about it before you answer, because your taste in vehicles tells a lot about you. For instance, the fact that Knox spends most of his time on the back of the black beast or in this over-sized hunk of metal suggests that he's overcompensating for . . ." he paused dramatically, "something."

Knox grunted. "At least I don't drive a soccer mom car."

I laughed, looking back and forth between the two of them; it was like watching a game of ping pong.

"Hey! It is the top-rated vehicle for cyclists, thank you very much! And don't distract me. This is about Haley." He turned back to me. "So?"

I thought for a few moments and finally said, "I don't know. I've never really thought about it. The only thing I've ever driven was my dad's truck, which was fine, but it wouldn't be my first choice."

"Well then, you can try out each of our vehicles and see what you like the best." Theo's smile widened, "I see you in something cute and sporty."

Knox shook his head. "Forget cute, she needs something safe and reliable. Maybe a Honda."

"Stop being such a stick-in-the-mud," Theo said. "We're talking about dream cars here, not grandma cars."

Wanting to stop their argument before it really started, I interrupted. "It's not like it matters. I can't afford a bicycle, much less a car, dream or otherwise." Theo started to protest, but I continued, "At least I know who to ask for advice when I'm eventually ready to look at cars."

My statement seemed to appease Theo for now, and he changed the subject. "I've decided that I'm going to climb El Gigante. I know things are busy right now, but I want to fit in more training when I can so that I'm ready by Christmas break." Theo's voice sounded unsure, almost like he was hoping Knox would give his permission.

Knox stared straight ahead, silent. I was tempted to duck behind the seat to make myself invisible. Clearly this conversation was not going to be pleasant.

Theo, obviously annoyed by Knox's reaction, or lack thereof, tauntingly said, "What? You don't think I can do it?"

Knox gruffly replied, "What do you want me to say, Theo? I've already told you that I don't want you to climb that stupid rock. It's not safe, and there's no reason for you to take that kind of risk, not only by climbing it, but also by traipsing off to a foreign country on your own."

"Oh, so it's fine for you to take a risk every time you get on your motorcycle or go kiteboarding? But I can't do the same? You're not my father, Knox. Stop treating me like a child!" *What is kiteboarding?* I tucked the question away for another time. There was no way I was going to speak right then; the air in the truck was already crackling with tension.

Knox's jaw clenched and his scowl was deeper than I'd ever seen it. "You're right. Unlike our father, I actually care what happens to you."

Theo hung his head. After a few moments, he quietly said, "I know, and I'm sorry. But I really wish you would start treating me like an equal. This is important to me."

Knox ran a hand through his hair and glanced back at me. "Can we talk about this later? Haley doesn't need to witness our family drama."

Theo laughed darkly. "She's living with us. She might as well get used to it."

Uncomfortable, I sat there quietly. I didn't know anything about their family, but clearly there was more to the story than two brothers living together.

Theo turned around and looked at me, his face unusually stoic. "You'll find out eventually, so I'll give you the CliffsNotes version now. Our dad has been out of the picture since we were young. Mom couldn't cope and was pretty much absent until she died. So, we've been taking care of ourselves for a long time. And, Knox likes to think that just because he's older, he's in charge." Theo turned back toward the front and stared out the windshield.

Knox tapped his hand on the steering wheel angrily. "Damn it, Theo. What is your problem? Do you really think this is the right time to get into all of that?" He gave me an apologetic look. "I'm sorry, Haley. Ignore him."

As awkward as the moment was, I found myself wanting to make sense of their family dynamics. It was clear that Knox was serious about his role as the protective older brother. And though Theo appeared to love and respect Knox, he was pushing back against Knox's self-imposed authority.

I probably should have stayed silent, but I couldn't help myself. "I'm sorry about your parents, but I'm also kind of jealous. You two are really lucky to have each other, to have someone that you can always count on."

Theo sighed. "You're right; we are lucky. Not just because we have each other, but because we have the team as well. It's like we make up our own little island of misfit orphans." He grinned, and I relaxed a little.

Ignoring his *Rudolph* reference for the moment, I asked, "Orphans? Does that mean that all of the guys on the team have parents who have died?" It occurred to me that as attached as I was feeling to Theo, Knox, Ethan, and Chase, I barely knew anything about their personal lives.

Knox responded, "Technically, no. But all of our parents have either died or deserted us in one way or another. That's why we are so close; despite our different backgrounds and personalities, our friendships were built on common ground." He paused and looked at me through the mirror. "Maybe now you can understand why it was so important to us to bring you to Santa Cruz and watch out for you."

Knox's green eyes burned into me, and I experienced a moment of clarity. The guys weren't helping me just because they felt responsible or guilty. They all had something significant in common with me and maybe even identified with me better than I ever imagined.

Turning off highway seventeen, we headed toward Saratoga. Not long after, we passed through a gated entrance, easily clearing the security booth before reaching a large fountain with lush ornamental landscaping. Theo said, "We're almost there."

As we drove further into the neighborhood, my jaw dropped. Enormous houses in all different styles were nestled in amongst the rolling hills. I tried to reassure myself that perhaps Jackson's uncle's house would be one of the smaller ones. "Does Jackson live here with his uncle?"

Knox replied, "Not since he finished college. Now he lives in a little bungalow right on the beach in Santa Cruz. It's perfect for surfing."

A minute or two later my conjectures were firmly put to rest when Knox pulled up to a large and elegant house. When he parked behind Chase's car, I gulped. Would it be obvious that I really didn't belong here?

Theo grabbed my canvas bag and his own duffel and opened my door. "Come on, Haley!" He smiled.

Considering I didn't really have any other choice, I silently followed Knox and Theo up the wide pathway toward the house. The landscaping was simple but pristine, mostly hedges and grass. The clean design of the landscaping complemented the large, two-story home. It reminded me of French chateaus I had seen in books at the library, complete with a beige stone facade, evenly-spaced tall windows, and a slate gray roof. Each of the upstairs windows were French doors with metal railings, and a large walk-out balcony was centered above the enormous front door.

Apart from the metal railing of the upper balconies, the front door was one of the most ornamental and decorative items on the house. As we approached the threshold, I admired the iron scrollwork design that covered the glass center of the arched doorway. I expected Knox to knock or ring the doorbell. Instead, he flipped a lid, revealing a small keypad into which he quickly entered a code, and then placed his thumb on a screen. My eyebrows raised so high I wasn't sure there was any space left on my forehead for them to go. If I hadn't already been wondering what exactly Jackson's uncle did for a living, I sure was now.

Entering the house, I was somewhat surprised that no one was there to greet us, but Theo and Knox seemed familiar with the home. Knox headed toward the back of the house, and I followed Theo up a nearby staircase, not sure what else to do.

I quickly surveyed the home as we traveled to an unknown destination within. Walking across beautiful tile floors, we passed large metal and crystal chandeliers, and upholstered furniture, curtains, and rugs in a variety of textures. Much like the exterior, the interior color palette was varying shades of gray and cream with live plants and flower arrangements sprinkled throughout. There was a definite air of luxury, but the overall effect was one of simplicity and understated elegance.

Theo stopped in front of a door on the upstairs hallway and opened it for me, revealing a bedroom. Nothing seemed very personal; it was clearly a guest bedroom. I assumed we were just ditching our stuff before heading back downstairs.

Theo set my bag on the bench at the foot of the bed. "Here you go, Haley. Since you didn't wear your swimsuit over, you can change in here or the attached bathroom. I'll be downstairs."

Curling my hair around my finger, I tried to remain calm, but I wanted to beg Theo to stay behind and wait for me. *Don't be ridiculous, Haley.* He smiled warmly, and I felt like he was trying to reassure me, so I nodded.

When he closed the door softly behind him, I glanced around. The late afternoon sun filtered through light and airy linen curtains, casting a warm glow about the room. The large bed had a headboard upholstered in dark gray and was covered in plush layers of beautiful bedding. A wood dresser that was both long and tall was topped with large lamps and decorative items. With a sense of slight disbelief at my beautiful surroundings, I leaned forward to smell the small arrangement of pink peonies.

Having seen glimpses of the house and now this guest room, I tried to think what it reminded me of. I felt a feel of smug sense of satisfaction when the answer came to me. There was a catalog we used to get that was as big as a phone book, always with a large "RH" on the cover. We could never figure out how they decided to include our address in their mailing list, having never purchased anything from the store. But, I loved poring over its glossy pages.

Knowing I really couldn't stall any longer, I sighed, pulling items out of my tote, including a new swimsuit. A few days ago, several swimsuits had appeared on my bed, and I picked two to keep but brought my favorite today.

I removed my clothes and stepped into the navy one-piece, shifting and pulling it up over my hips and torso. After moving my long hair to one side, I tied the slick fabric in a bow to create the halter-neck. I loved the retro feel of the suit thanks to the ruching on the front, twisted bust, and boyshorts cut of the bottom. I shook my head at Theo's uncanny knack for picking clothes for me; somehow I felt covered yet sexy.

I threw on a cover-up before pulling my hair into a high ponytail. A few tendrils hung around my face, refusing to stay back. Finally grabbing a book and placing my sunglasses on my head, I took a deep breath and opened the door. *Theo said he would be downstairs, but who else is here? Jackson? Ethan?* I wasn't sure who I was most anxious to see or not see.

I descended the stairs slowly, keeping an ear out for the others while continuing to admire the design of the home. Assuming the pool was located at the back of the house, I headed in that direction. When I heard Knox's voice, I relaxed slightly and felt brave enough to pop my head around the corner to investigate.

Knox was sitting on a bar stool in the kitchen talking to a man whom I'd never seen before. The stranger was facing mostly away from me with one hip leaning against the counter, his stance confident yet relaxed. He was wearing what must have been an expensive suit in deep blue with a white dress shirt, open at the neck.

Knox spotted me and said, "Hey, Haley. Come meet Liam." Wishing I could dodge behind the wall, I knew it was too late.

Liam turned around and immediately started toward me. "Haley, we meet at last." Surprised by the sound of a light British accent rolling off his tongue, I stood frozen. He stopped a short distance away from me and looked me up and down, his intent unmistakable. "Well you're bloody gorgeous, aren't you?" Glancing back at Knox, he said, "Now I can see why you've been hiding her at the loft."

My cheeks immediately began to burn, making my discomfort obvious. While Theo and Ethan made statements now and then that were moderately flirtatious, they had nothing on Liam. Something about the bold look in his eyes mixed with the smooth tone of his voice made his words seem anything but innocent. While I might have been getting used to hanging out with the other guys, Liam was a completely new creature, and I had no idea what to do with him.

He held out his hand and I placed mine in his, expecting a simple handshake. Instead, he slowly drew my hand up to his lips and placed a light kiss on the back of my hand. "I am Liam Carlyle. It is lovely to meet you." I didn't know whether to be impressed or repelled. Movies and novels taught me that a kiss on the hand was the swoon-worthy act of a gentleman. But, I was fighting a laugh, because it just seemed so over-the-top and cheesy. *Is he always like this?*

Nevertheless, I couldn't deny that he was incredibly attractive. Like the rest of the guys on the team, he could pass for a model or even a movie star. He was about the same height as Knox but much slimmer. His expertly tailored suit fit him perfectly, showing off his trim physique. Combined with his height and the elegant way he carried himself, he looked like he owned the place; there was an air of insouciance about him.

He had dark brown hair that was cut short and styled to perfection. With prominent cheekbones and a rather deep dimple in his chin, his otherwise smooth face was a study of lines and angles. And when he smiled, I couldn't help but be dazzled by his brilliant white teeth.

Realizing that I'd been standing there staring at him, I finally said, "The guys mentioned you, but I didn't realize you were British. Unless the accent is fake," I added with a grin.

Liam laughed, his entire face lighting up as he smiled. For the first time, I noticed the unusual color of his eyes. They were gray but seemed to change colors from one moment to the next.

"We're going to hit it off, I can already tell." He walked back to Knox and said, "I like her."

Knox watched both of us with a warm look in his eyes. "I know."

Jumping In

As I lounged by the pool, I couldn't get over my lush surroundings. The back of Jackson's uncle's house was even more beautiful than the front, thanks in no small part to the pool and landscaping. A covered outdoor patio, attached to the house, flowed seamlessly into the tiled patio and flawless green lawn surrounding the pool.

The lounge chair beneath me almost felt too nice to be outdoor furniture. Caressing the plush fabric of the cushion, I admired the large rectangular pool that stretched tantalizingly before me. With its simple design and clear blue water, it was perfect for swimming laps. I closed my eyes, inhaling deeply and soaking in the warmth of the sun. Apart from the faint scent of chlorine, the air smelled clean and pure.

Opening my eyes, I marveled at how expansive, and yet sheltered, the space felt. A border of shrubs and beautiful white hydrangeas outlined segments of the pool and lawn before the yard faded into a larger, more natural wooded area. With trees all around and no other houses in sight, it was quite the serene oasis.

A book sat open on my lap, but it was more for cover than for reading. Theo and Chase were already in the pool swimming laps, and I had successfully avoided their attempts to lure me in thus far. The only people who had seen me in a swimsuit were Jessica and my dad, and the thought of shedding my cover-up in front of the guys was making me more than a little anxious.

As I watched Theo and Chase swimming, I was impressed by their skills. However, it was clear that Chase was the superior swimmer, and I understood why swimming was his chosen sport. He was expertly performing the breaststroke, and the way his limbs elegantly sliced through the water was hypnotizing.

The sound of the patio door sliding open caught my attention, and I glanced over my shoulder, expecting Knox and Liam. Instead, Ethan appeared in a pair of horizontally-striped swim trunks, a towel draped over one shoulder. My heart started beating wildly, and I quickly turned away to keep from gawking at his incredible musculature. *Please don't come over here, please don't come over here.*

Luckily, Theo caught Ethan's attention by hopping out of the pool and heading straight toward him. He grabbed Ethan's towel and threw it on a nearby chair. "Haley gets a pass for now, but you don't, so get your butt in the pool."

Ethan followed Theo to the edge of the pool but hesitated for a moment, looking over at me. Thankful for the sunglasses hiding my eyes, I kept my head down but watched him out of the corner of my eye. He started to say something, but before he had the chance, Theo pushed him in the pool. Once he broke through the surface of the water, he initiated a splash war against Theo and had Chase in the middle within seconds.

I watched, amused by their playfulness and relieved that I managed to avoid a conversation with Ethan for a while longer. I intended to finally confront him about the phone call sometime tonight but wanted to wait until I could talk to him alone.

For now, I let myself enjoy the moment. Constantly in motion, their muscles flexing and the sun highlighting their bodies, the water streamed off them, and the effect was breathtaking. *Had the fire been a portal to an alternate Abercrombie-&-Fitch-catalog universe?*

By the time Liam and Knox came outside a few minutes later, the guys had called a truce. As Liam walked by, he held out a hand, palm up. "Oh, Haley. Do please join us."

I shook my head and smiled as I held up my book. Liam wasn't backing down easily though. "Seriously? Surely even the incomparable Mr. Darcy can't compete with the five of us?" Was he mocking my reading selection? *Pride and Prejudice* was a classic, with a cult following that even went so far as to include a zombie parody.

Affecting my best English accent and serious manner, I replied. "My dear Mr. Carlyle, I must respectfully decline your request." He laughed before walking off and glanced back at me once more before diving effortlessly into the pool.

Theo swam to the edge of the pool near my lounge chair. "Please, Haley. We need you to make our numbers even for basketball."

I rolled my eyes behind my sunglasses but held my ground. "I'm sure I would hurt, not help, whichever team I was on. I've never even played basketball."

Theo glared. "Oh please; we both know you can easily pick it up. Don't make me come out and get you." He flicked water playfully in my direction. "You know I will."

Realizing that I wasn't going to get away with staying dry forever, I finally gave in and set my book down on the chair. As I stood up and prepared to remove my cover-up, I felt like time was standing still. I took a few deep breaths and gave myself a quick pep talk. *Chill, Haley, you can do this. It's just a bathing suit.* Refusing to make eye contact with anyone, I slowly slipped the cover-up over my head before placing it and my sunglasses on the lounge chair.

At first there was complete silence from the direction of the pool, but then I heard Ethan's deep voice mutter, "Damn," his tone sounding a bit awed. Knowing that I had to face them at some point, I turned to the guys and slowly walked to the pool steps.

Theo beamed up at me. "I hoped you would pick that one; it looks amazing on you." I ducked my head to hide my blush and concentrated on entering the pool without tripping or doing something else equally embarrassing. The water felt cool and refreshing, and I sighed at the pleasure of it washing over my warm skin.

Next, I heard Liam say, "*You* picked out that suit? Why couldn't you have bought her a bikini?" Uncomfortable and slightly annoyed, I looked up to see Knox smack Liam on the back of the head, making all the other guys laugh.

While I paddled around, Theo said, "Okay, let's pick teams."

Theo opened his mouth again to speak, but Knox butted in. "Yes, let's. Ethan and I will pick." He paused for half a second. "I'll go first. Haley." Knox's tone was friendly, but there was a definite undercurrent of authority. Even though I knew it was a pity pick, I felt relieved that I wasn't chosen last.

Ethan groaned but didn't protest. "Fine, I'll take Chase." It suddenly struck me why Ethan looked different; he wasn't wearing his glasses. I had a hard time deciding whether he looked better with or without them.

Knox quickly said, "Theo," before Ethan said, "Come on, Liam."

Theo and Chase hopped out of the pool, dripping water as their bare feet pattered across the patio tile, returning with two basketball goals and a ball. While they set up the goals, Ethan quickly went over the rules. "Okay, no traveling, aka swimming, beyond one-quarter length of the pool at one time with the ball. You can't take the ball out of the pool. Blocking is allowed, but you can't push someone under water and hold them there. Once a team scores, we meet at the center and start again. Any violation means a free throw. Got it?"

Everyone nodded. Knox was standing near me and moved closer. "Any questions?" I shook my head. He smoothed his wet hair back from his face. Lowering his head near mine, he practically whispered in my ear. "Good. I picked you as my ringer; don't let them push you around." Maybe I wasn't picked out of pity after all? Although "ringer" definitely seemed like wishful thinking.

With the goals set up at each end of the pool, Chase flipped a coin. Our team won the coin toss, so we got the ball first. Having seen them splashing around in the pool earlier, I was worried I wouldn't be able to keep up, but I was determined to at least try.

Knox shouted, "Go," and it felt as if all hell had broken loose. While I stayed where I was, the boys sprang into action, each swimming quickly toward a member of the opposite team. The water churned from the motion, and waves lapped at the edge of the pool. Knox was dancing around with Ethan near the center of the pool, and Theo swam toward our goal with Liam in hot pursuit.

Chase appeared in front of me. "Hi, Haley." He grinned before turning his back on me.

Standing in front of me with his arms spread, Chase didn't have to do much to block me, especially as distracted as I was by his incredible shoulders. Knowing he had the advantage, I thought maybe diverting his attention was a better tactic. "Hey, Chase?"

"Mhmm." Darn, his back was still turned.

"Chase." I said louder and with more emphasis. I knew it was a dirty trick, but I had to be creative if I was going to have any chance. He turned around and I ducked under his arms quickly, swimming in front of him while he turned. Knox saw what I had done and threw the ball in my direction. The ball hit the water in front of me, making a plonking noise and splashing before I clutched it to my chest.

Feeling my legs being pulled away from me, I kicked furiously while glancing around the pool for Knox and Theo. Fortunately, Knox managed to swim closer to me despite having Ethan close behind. I shoved the ball at Knox before going under completely. When I popped back up, Theo had the ball. The guys moved swiftly in the water, and I did my best to keep up with them and the ball.

I swam in Theo's direction, but before I could get there, Liam had stolen the ball from him. With Theo behind Liam, and Knox on the other side of the pool with Ethan, Chase and I were in the center of the action. Chase was a fast swimmer, and I had already tricked him once. I didn't think I could get away with it again. *What can I do?*

Liam was headed our way at full speed, and I had the harebrained idea to try and stop him. I pushed off the side of the pool with my feet, hoping I would T-bone him at just the right moment. Despite the impact, he managed to hang on to the ball and raised it high above his head, looking for someone to pass it to.

By then, Theo had caught up to us and was blocking Chase while I had Liam. I waved my arms like crazy while jumping up and down, just hoping to distract him with my crazy antics, if nothing else. He laughed, but between me guarding him and Theo guarding Chase, they were stuck.

Liam's smile was electric, and he moved with grace and strength. Even without the expensive clothes tailored to his frame, there was an elegance to him. But with his hair wet and messy and his absorption in the game, he seemed cuter, almost goofy, even.

Ethan finally got away from Knox, and Liam flung the ball in his direction. Ethan caught it and shot a goal, scoring to the loud cheers of Liam and Chase. "One, nothing," Ethan said, smirking.

Ethan, Chase, and Liam gave a round of high fives as we all swam back to the center of the pool to restart. Everyone was trash-talking at this point, and Liam flashed me a smug grin. "Guess you'll just have to try harder next time." His gray eyes reflected the blue water and danced in the sunlight. *He's challenging me; I'll show him.*

Chase swam up behind us. "You play a good game, Haley. But your team hasn't scored yet."

I smiled. "The key word is yet." I dove underwater, resurfacing near the center of the pool. *Okay, Haley. You can do this.* Knox's words rang in my ear. *Don't let them push you around.*

Ethan held the ball and shouted, "Go!" Fortunately, I was more prepared this time and immediately headed in Liam's direction. Doing my best to block him, I moved non-stop in an effort to prevent him from getting the ball. When Ethan tried to pass the ball to Chase, Knox managed to hit it, pushing it off course from its intended target. Everyone beelined for the ball, but Theo got there first.

Theo shouted my name and lifted his chin in the direction of the goal. I swam as fast as I could toward our goal. When Theo threw the ball my direction, I lunged and grabbed it. My heart was racing and I knew I was close to the goal, but Liam moved through the water like a shark.

After he quickly snatched the ball from me and turned to go the opposite direction, I jumped on his back. I clung to Liam and held on for dear life as he struggled to get away. It wasn't long before he stopped swimming and stood twisting from side to side while I attempted to stop him or release the ball. I was doing my best to hold him back, but he was clearly enjoying himself.

Finally, out of instinct, I reached around his sides. I tickled his ribs and he started laughing. "Haley, stop that!" I laughed, breathless from the exertion and the excitement, but didn't stop.

I was too busy distracting Liam to focus on where the other guys were. Suddenly a strong arm reached around my waist, pulling me beneath the surface. A second arm wrapped around me, embracing me. Unprepared, I hadn't taken a breath and my lungs were burning. I pried his arms open, releasing me to move to the surface. *I. Need. Air.*

As I swam upward, I was fighting the pain in my lungs and the urge to cough. It felt like I couldn't get air fast enough. When I finally surfaced, I immediately started coughing and gasping for air. The others stopped what they were doing and turned to look at me as Knox quickly came to my side.

Knox looked concerned. "Just breathe, Haley. You're okay. Relax." He spoke slowly and his tone was soothing.

Once I caught my breath again, he smoothed a few strands of hair away from my face. "You okay?"

I closed my eyes and nodded. "I'll be fine."

When Knox turned on Ethan, I could feel the anger radiating from him. His voice was level, but there was a definite edge to it. "What the hell do you think you were doing?"

Ethan straightened. "Playing the game. What's the big deal?"

Knox glared at him. "No. You were too aggressive."

I spoke in a hoarse voice. "I'm fine, Knox. Let's just play." Knox's shoulders relaxed slightly, and he turned away from Ethan to face me. "You sure?"

I smiled. "You sure you want to just end it now and let them win?"

Theo grinned. "That's my girl. Now let's stop talking and play!"

Chase jumped in front of me, ready to guard. Ethan swam by, his eyes apologetic and questioning.

Despite our best efforts, my team lost by two points. While I wasn't the ringer Knox hoped for, I had to admit to having fun; and I had even scored a goal. However, given a choice of games, I would probably go with poker instead. The guys were extremely competitive, and playing in the water for so long was exhausting.

After the game's conclusion, Theo started another water fight by splashing me lightly in the face. Almost simultaneously, Chase, Ethan, and Liam attacked Theo while Knox pulled me out of the way and blocked me with his body.

When their playful fighting turned aggressive, Knox grabbed me by the waist and lifted me out of the pool, setting me gently on the tile. With a sheepish grin, he said, "Go dry off. You don't want to get in the middle of this," before disappearing under the water.

Relieved to be out of the line of fire, I used one of the luxurious beach towels to dry off. Since it appeared that the guys weren't quitting anytime soon, I pulled my cover-up on over my soaked swimsuit and headed inside to change.

I opened one side of the French doors and slipped inside, the cool air making me shiver. When I saw a slight movement out of the corner of my eye, I jumped, clumsily dropping my towel and book.

Jackson stood leaning against the large window next to the door, arms crossed over his chest. He was still dressed in work clothes but had a distinctly casual air about him in linen slacks paired with a white button-down shirt.

His lips tipped into a barely-there smile. "Haley, we really need to stop meeting like this. Are you always so jumpy?"

Intimidated by his presence, I reached down to pick up my things to avoid his gaze. "Not usually.

It must be you." *Geez, Haley, why are you such a nervous wreck around him?*

When he didn't reply, I finally looked at him and he lifted one dark brow. "Well then, I apologize."

I bit my lip, trying to come up with an intelligent response. When nothing came to mind, I decided to change the subject. "Have you heard anything about the office assistant position? Do you know when I'm going to start?"

Jackson stood up straight and placed his hands in his pockets. "Yes, everything is ready to go. You can start as early as next week if you'd like."

My pulse started to race in excitement. "Really? That would be great."

He consulted his phone for a few moments before returning his attention to me, his voice as professional as ever. "It looks like my schedule is fairly clear on Monday if you would like to start then."

Suddenly Monday seemed alarmingly close, and I felt a twinge of fear at having to face new people and circumstances in just a couple of days. Then I reminded myself that not only had I desired this type of opportunity for years, I needed to start saving money as soon as possible.

At the moment, my best shot at finding my dad depended on getting to San Francisco and accessing the safe deposit box. At the very least, I needed enough cash for bus fare and a few nights in a hotel. But I preferred to wait until I had the resources to make it on my own for an extended period of time.

"Of course, whenever is most convenient for you." I hoped he could tell how grateful I was for setting up the job.

Jackson slid his phone back in his pocket and said, "Okay, Monday morning it is. I'm sure Theo or Knox will be able to give you a ride."

I glanced outside and saw the guys exiting the pool. Realizing this was the perfect time to escape, I said, "Thank you so much. I better go change before I freeze."

Jackson politely offered, "Please let me know if you need anything. Did someone already show you to a guest room?"

"Yes, thank you." I quickly turned and headed toward the staircase. As I made my way back to my designated room, I wondered how the rest of the evening would unfold. *One down, one to go.* I had managed to get the easy conversation out of the way; now I just had to get Ethan alone and confront him. I needed answers, and fast; I was getting way too close to these guys, especially considering Ethan's apparent betrayal.

I sucked in a quick breath at the thought of the guys downstairs. All six were insanely attractive, worldly, and smart. And I was so . . . sheltered. At that moment, confronting Ethan almost seemed like the least of my worries. *How will I ever survive this evening?*

Lucky Number Seven

Padding down the back stairs to the kitchen, I shouldn't have been surprised at the scene that greeted me. Liam stood at the kitchen counter with a pile of vegetables while I watched, mesmerized by his expert chopping. His long, elegant fingers moved with grace and precision as he wielded the sharp knife like a surgeon.

Out the glass patio doors, I could see Knox and Jackson behind the huge stainless steel grill. Even in the relaxed setting, Jackson still seemed so reserved. *Surely he lets loose sometimes?*

Knox, on the other hand, stood barefoot at the grill, giant tongs in one hand, drink in another. And Chase, Theo, and Ethan were in the yard throwing a Frisbee. After all of my interactions with them, I should have known they wouldn't be stereotypical guys who ordered pizza and sat around drinking beer on a Friday night.

As I walked into the kitchen, Liam lifted his head and shot me a devilish grin while giving me another once-over. "What lovely hair you have. You really should wear it like that all the time." *Why do I feel like I'm looking at a frustratingly hot version of the Big Bad Wolf?*

Ignoring the compliment, I nervously ran a hand over my hair, trying to smooth it down. After quickly washing my hair to get rid of the chlorine, I had dried it for just a few minutes, and now it hung down my back in an array of messy waves. Between my hair and comfortable shorts and T-shirt, I was particularly aware of how casual I looked in comparison to Liam.

While the other guys wore some variation of jeans, shorts, and T-shirts or polos, Liam's version of "casual" was somewhat formal, thanks to his pressed shorts and button-down shirt with the sleeves rolled up. Not to mention the unusual gold ring on his pinky; a simple band with a flat oval face, it appeared to be engraved.

Hoping to change the subject from my appearance, I walked up to the counter and asked, "Is there anything I can do to help?"

"No. You can help yourself to a drink, though. There's even beer in the fridge," he said, tilting his head toward the refrigerator. Okay, maybe I was wrong about the guys drinking beer.

Knox walked in during Liam's statement and frowned. "No underage drinking, Liam. You know Uncle's rules." He opened the refrigerator and pulled out a glass pitcher with slices of lemon floating at the top. "Lemonade?"

"Absolutely. It looks delicious." I was relieved that Knox saved me from responding about the beer. I had never tried it and really had no interest in doing so tonight.

Liam popped a piece of pineapple in his mouth, chewing as he resumed chopping fruit. Since he was doing all the prep work for the dinner, it seemed only fair that he should get to snitch some. When he realized he had been caught, he smirked and held a piece out to me, eyebrows raised in silent invitation.

I gave him a sly grin before accepting the pineapple; its sweetness exploded instantly on my tongue. After our strenuous basketball game, I was ravenous. I poured my drink and then followed Knox outside, the smell from the grill teasing me.

When I sat down at an outdoor dining table, Chase ambled over and pulled out the chair next to me. "May I?"

"Hmmm . . ." I tapped my finger on my chin like I had to think about it. "Considering our basketball rivalry, that may be a little too close." I smiled, letting him know that I was teasing.

Chase laughed softly and plopped down in the seat. "If it makes you feel any better, you were a worthy opponent, especially considering it was your first time to play."

I quirked an eyebrow. "If by worthy, you mean underhanded, then sure."

Chase just shook his head with a grin, a dimple appearing in one cheek. "Good point. By the way, Jackson mentioned that you're starting work next week. Do you feel ready?" He looked at me thoughtfully, his sky blue eyes revealing his concern.

I huffed a quiet sigh. "Honestly, I'm not sure. Part of me is excited to finally interact with others like a normal member of society. The other part of me is terrified that being around more new people will be completely overwhelming and awkward." Sharing this with Chase seemed natural, even though I knew most people couldn't relate.

His expression serious, Chase said, "I totally understand where you're coming from; I still get overwhelmed in new situations, and I've had a lot more practice. But, I'm confident you'll fit in at Zenith. And at least one of us will always be around, so you have nothing to worry about."

Grateful for his reassurance, I nodded. "You're right. And I'm really glad that Jackson was willing to set me up with a job at Zenith." I glanced over at Jackson and was shocked to see him looking laid back, smiling and laughing with the other guys. If I didn't know better, I would think he was a completely different person.

"I'm a little surprised, really. I don't think he likes me."

Chase appeared confused. "Who, Jackson?"

I nodded. "He was really standoffish both times I've talked to him. But seeing him now, I think it must be me."

Chase studied Jackson for a moment before replying. "I don't think it's you specifically. Jackson is extremely protective of our team; I'm sure he'll warm up once he gets to know you."

Before I had time to ponder the idea more, Theo interrupted. "No more gossiping, you two. Time to eat!"

Our plates piled high, I joined Knox, Liam, and Jackson at the table just outside the pool house. A gentle breeze blew through the backyard, and I couldn't imagine a more perfect temperature or setting.

Jackson cut into his steak before addressing me. "Well, Haley, did you enjoy the game? I hope they played nice."

I smiled, brushing my wet hair behind my shoulder. "Nice enough." I grinned. "I had fun."

Jackson spoke again. "I'm glad to see they're making you feel welcome."

I nodded. "They definitely are." I paused. "And, thank you for including me tonight." *Not that you really had a choice considering I'm a pseudo-prisoner*, I thought. It seemed best left unsaid, especially considering how much I was enjoying my present situation.

Liam opened his mouth in feigned surprise. "Unbelievable." He paused dramatically. "Haley is so polite, so well-mannered with you. Yet, Miss Manners had the audacity to question the authenticity of my accent within moments of our introduction." He looked at me, the light dancing in his gray eyes.

Jackson chuckled. "You have lived here for over half your life, so it is somewhat surprising your accent hasn't faded more. Perhaps it really is just an act for the ladies."

Liam dramatically rolled his eyes. "I can't help it if they find my accent sexy."

Knox threw back the rest of his drink before adding. "Your accent or your Audi?"

Jackson chuckled and closed his eyes briefly while he shook his head. "You know, Uncle often says that your accent just gets you into trouble. And I think I'm beginning to agree." He smirked, clearly enjoying the verbal banter with Liam.

Liam's eyes gleamed, and I couldn't shake the image of a panther on the prowl. "What rubbish. Do you realize how many times my accent has saved your arse?" He grinned and then pursed his lips. "Hmm. Jealousy, perhaps?"

Jackson wasn't going to let that slide. "And do you know how many more I've saved your arse?"

I smiled at their antics; it was clear they were joking and enjoying themselves. I wondered how long they had been friends, especially since their bond seemed deeper, almost like brothers.

Liam reached his long fingers toward Jackson's neck. Jackson looked down and noticed that part of his collar had flapped up; he gently flipped it even further out of place. "Something wrong?" I saw the hint of a grin play at the corner of Jackson's lips.

Jackson reached for Liam's head, threatening the perfectly styled hair, but Liam quickly ducked out of the way. "Don't even think about it, Jax," his tone playful, yet serious. Apart from Liam, I had only ever heard Knox use "Jax." *Interesting*.

As I finished my meal, I enjoyed the overwhelming sense of relaxation and content that spread over me. In need of a refill, I headed inside the pool house to grab more water.

With the doors open to the backyard, the pool house formed part of a seamless whole with the main house and the backyard. Decorated in the same style, it was more casual and definitely cozier. With one bedroom, one bathroom, and a living room, it was really just a fun space for the guys to hang out. A wet bar and small fridge served as the kitchen, and with a grill just outside next to the table and chairs, it seemed like the ideal location. Good thing there was no "Boys Only" rule to this clubhouse. I wondered how many outsiders were invited to this more intimate and private setting.

Chase and Ethan sat on the plush, over-sized sofas eating and watching the television; Theo held the remote, absent-mindedly flipping channels.

Occasionally he would linger on one, but he was clicking so rapidly, I wondered how he could even tell if the program was something he was interested in.

Even Chase seemed impatient. "Come on, Theo. You know the game is on channel twenty-two. Can't we just watch that?"

Theo laughed. "Don't be silly; we have to survey all the options first."

When he stopped on a telenovela, Ethan groaned and tried to steal the remote. Theo kept the remote out of reach and said, "Wait, wait. I want to see this."

On the screen was a beautiful but angry woman and a forlorn-looking man. They were arguing, and I had to concentrate to keep up with their fast-paced Spanish dialogue.

Theo laughed and said, "This is great." He focused on the television and then started translating the dialogue in English, his voice taking on a believable accent with added flair to amp up the melodrama.

"Fernando, I know you slept with Adriana! I will never forgive you!"

"I'm sorry, Gabriela, just let me explain. It wasn't my fault."

"I don't want to hear your pathetic excuses. Get away from me! I never want to see you again!"

"But how could I have known that she was your twin? You never even told me you had a sister!"

Theo mimicked both of the characters perfectly, and I couldn't help but laugh. He was undoubtedly fluent in Spanish . . . like Ethan. As the thought crossed my mind, I found myself speaking, not taking the time to consider whether it was a good idea.

Attempting only a slight Spanish accent, I spoke Gabriela's next line. "I didn't tell you because Adriana was supposed to be dead! I wish she was!"

I felt every eye in the room turn to stare at me. Theo gave me a huge grin, nodding as he continued. "How could you say that about your own twin?"

Not wanting to give up on the game, I continued Gabriela's part, translating the best that I could. "Because she is the evil twin. She deserved to die in that hurricane. I can't believe she survived on a stranded island for the past five years."

The show went to commercial and several of the guys started clapping. Theo took a bow and said, "Haley, that was awesome. I didn't know you speak Spanish."

I hesitated for a moment and then looked directly into Ethan's eyes. "I'm not fluent, but I know enough to understand most of what I hear or read."

Ethan stared back and me, his face stoic. I wondered if he could feel the current of anger I was channeling toward him. If he wasn't suspicious that I was upset with him before, he definitely should be now.

By this point, Knox, Liam, and Jackson had migrated into the pool house, ready for the feature film. Nothing was said about the seating arrangements, but they all instinctively seemed to know where to sit. Chase patted the space on a sofa between himself and Knox. I wasn't sure the three of us would fit comfortably, but it seemed preferable to the tile floor, even with the rug.

And I couldn't deny that the idea of being snuggled up between Chase and Knox was appealing. I knew I was in over my head, but I just couldn't resist the temptation. *Besides*, I thought, *is it really such a big deal to sit between them on the couch?*

Jackson grabbed the remote and stood in front of the TV. "Okay, what do you guys . . ." he paused, "And girl, want to watch tonight?"

Liam laughed. "Well this is a first. Although considering the quality time the rest of you have spent with her, it seems only fair that Haley should sit with me."

Jackson rolled his eyes but continued talking, proposing a few movie options. Theo threw out a few horror films, but Knox shook his head. I couldn't imagine that Knox would be afraid of anything, let alone a movie; I wondered if he vetoed them for my benefit. Several of the guys spoke up, naming films I had never heard of — *Fight Club; Lock, Stock, & Two Smoking Barrels; Monty Python and the Holy Grail*. Some of the suggestions were met with groans, but nothing seemed to be a clear winner.

Finally, Jackson picked a film and put it in the DVD; after the previews, the title *The Minority Report* flashed on the screen. Nestled in between Knox and Chase, I tried to relax and enjoy the movie, but all I could focus on was their legs and arms brushing against mine. I shook my head in disbelief at the situation. *Am I really watching a futuristic, sci-fi movie surrounded by six insanely attractive guys?* Any one of them alone was enough to make my heart flutter, but all together . . . I wasn't even sure how to finish that thought.

The sun had set and with the doors still open to the pool, I was getting cold in my linen shorts and V-neck T-shirt. At some point, Knox put his arm on the back of the couch and encouraged me to lean into him if I needed more space. I resisted at first but ever so slowly came to rest against him. His body was warm and comforting despite the hard muscles beneath his soft shirt.

The movie was engaging and the suspense intensified as it progressed. I could feel my anxiety rising as the main character dashed through the city, attempting to evade the police and the eye scans required for everything from entering a mall to making a purchase. Suddenly, a large, warm hand clapped over my eyes, obscuring my view. Surprised by the unexpected contact, I nearly jumped out of my skin.

With Knox's broad chest behind me and his arm curved around me, it felt like he was giving me a hug. His voice spoke reassuringly into my ear. "Trust me, Haley. You don't want to see this."

I whispered back. "Why not? I can handle it."

I gently nudged him in the ribs with my elbow, prodding him to let me see the screen. He spread his fingers slightly, allowing me a limited view.

"Ack! You're right." I clamped my eyes shut beneath his fingers, wishing I could erase even the brief image from my mind. I felt nauseated at the thought of eye replacement surgery. Knox patted me on the shoulder, and I could feel the light movement of his chest while he laughed gently.

At the end of *Minority Report*, I was left with a number of questions and the need for a quick trip to the bathroom. A baseball game played on the TV as I headed down the hall. Finishing up in the bathroom, I dried my hands on the towel before flipping off the light.

After the bright light of the bathroom, the hall seemed even darker while my eyes adjusted. I turned toward the living room, but a large hand grabbed my own and pulled me in the direction of the bedroom; I was moving so fast my hair whipped through the air.

Startled, I found myself standing face-to-face with Ethan as he closed the door behind us. Even in the dim light of the room, I could make out his facial expression, and he didn't look pleased. He held onto my hand a moment longer than necessary, and my heart began to race.

In the Dark

Ethan stood in the bedroom, his large frame overwhelming in the small room. "What was that about earlier?" His deep voice rumbled even though he was speaking softly.

Crossing my arms over my stomach, I took a deep breath and reminded myself to stay strong. I had been avoiding this confrontation for too long. I had imagined and rehearsed the conversation in my head for the past week, but he caught me by surprise. Now that the moment was actually here, I wasn't sure what to say. And I wasn't sure this was the time or place to say it, with the rest of the guys just on the other side of the wall.

I shrugged my shoulders. Did he really not get what this was about?

His eyes narrowed, assessing me. "Are you upset about what happened in the pool? I didn't mean to be so rough."

I shook my head. "No, it's not about the pool." *Just get it over with, Haley.*

I took a deep breath. "It's about trust." I saw a shift in Ethan's eyes as I continued speaking. "I opened up to you and shared things about my past, things that were personal. I thought I could trust you."

Ethan adjusted his glasses, his brown eyes full of concern. "You can trust me, Haley."

My whisper sounded harsh, each syllable staccato and over-pronounced. "You keep saying that, but how am I supposed to believe you when you're not being honest with me?" Ethan raised an eyebrow. Either he really didn't know what I was upset about, or he had an even better poker face than Knox.

"I heard you talking in Spanish on the last day at the cabin." I paused, hoping I could keep my voice from trembling. "I want you to explain."

Ethan did not visibly react to my statement. "You're going to have to tell me what you heard, because I don't remember that entire conversation off the top of my head."

"Basically, I heard you say that Chase had convinced me to come with you guys to Santa Cruz and that I wouldn't if I knew about something. It wasn't much, but it was enough to be make me suspicious." I crossed my arms over my chest, bracing for the answer.

"First of all, it was never our intention to keep this from you long-term. But we were worried if you found out, you would run. And we really are trying to protect you. Please hear me out."

I gave a belligerent nod before he continued. "After days of investigating, we were able to uncover that our client hired the men who were chasing your dad the day of the fire." My breath caught in my chest, and I looked toward the door, fighting an overwhelming desire to flee.

I hadn't realized how close I was to the bedroom wall until Ethan raised his arm, placing his hand on the wall beside my head, effectively blocking my exit. He leaned toward me, the space between our faces mere inches. I tried to listen to what Ethan was saying; I needed to know what was going on, but he was making it challenging to focus.

"We haven't revealed that we know this to our client because we are still trying to put the pieces together. Since he hasn't let us know that his men were on the scene, he's clearly hiding something. But we aren't sure of his intentions yet, and we can't assume that he plans to harm your dad. We need more information."

I let his words sink in. They made sense given the part of his conversation that I overheard. It was true that I probably wouldn't have agreed if I had known. I wouldn't have trusted that they were more concerned with my interests than their client's. Ironically, I didn't agree anyway because I didn't know the truth. Thus, the kidnapping.

"I wish you would have told me. It's already hard enough to trust all of you without knowing that you're keeping important information from me." I stared into his eyes, urging him to recognize how frustrated I was. "I'm tired of being kept in the dark. First my dad and now you. I don't want to live like that anymore."

He softened his voice. "I know, and I'm sorry. You have to understand that we work in a business that relies on confidentiality and secrecy. It's difficult to balance that against what we want to share with you."

He searched my face with his piercing gaze. "Forgive me?"

I hesitated a moment before nodding. His explanation made sense, and the truth was, I had missed Ethan and didn't want to hold onto a grudge. But more importantly, I knew the guys were looking out for me; I just didn't always agree with their methods.

Still leaning against the wall, Ethan used his free hand to brush my hair away from my face before gently trailing it down my cheek. The air between us was charged with electricity, and I felt breathless.

Embarrassed by how long I had been "in the bathroom," I figured it was time to rejoin the group. "We should probably get back." Ethan nodded, but I sensed some hesitation, and I realized that I didn't want our conversation to end on this note.

Placing my hand on the door knob, I paused. "You know, there's still something you haven't told me." I kept my tone serious.

Ethan looked concerned. "What's that?"

"Your last name," I said with a grin.

His shoulders dropped and one corner of his mouth turned up. "Wright." His smile grew. "Feel free to call me Mr. Wright."

Unsure whether he was teasing, I just shook my head with a laugh and turned to go. I had barely stepped into the short hallway before I was pulled backward, flush against Ethan's body. Enveloped in his arms, I felt warm and safe. I hesitantly wrapped my arms around his back and inwardly gasped at the feeling of his hard body against mine.

He dipped his head slightly and whispered into my ear as he held me. "Now that you're in Santa Cruz, I was really hoping we could go stargazing." I grinned from ear to ear, nodding into his chest, and he gently squeezed me in response.

I heard the sound of a throat clearing. "Everything okay?" Knox's rough voice filled the hall, and I guiltily pulled away from Ethan.

Why do I feel so uncomfortable? It was just a hug, right? "Yeah, everything is fine." I gave Ethan a small smile.

"Good," Knox said as he wrapped an arm around my shoulder and ushered me back to the living room.

Despite my desire to slip on the couch unnoticed, Theo exclaimed, "Haley, you're back!" His grin looked even more mischievous than normal, and I wondered what he was holding behind his back. "Are you ready?"

I furrowed my brow. "Ready for . . .?"

Theo pulled a large plastic gun from behind his back. "Outdoor laser tag!" He said it with such enthusiasm that I couldn't help but be a little excited at the idea.

I laughed. "If everyone else is playing, I guess so."

"Put this on," Chase said, handing me a large vest with plastic spots that I assumed were targets for the laser gun. The other guys grabbed vests and guns while Chase talked. "We picked teams; you're with Jackson, Ethan, and me. Aim for the targets or the gun. Try to hit them as many times as possible and don't get hit yourself. If you do get hit, you have to wait thirty seconds before you can shoot anyone again. But they can keep shooting you during those thirty seconds, so it's best to hide."

He smiled. "Just stick near Jackson, Ethan, or me. Don't worry; it will be fun."

Heading outdoors, I could feel the nervous excitement building within me. It was cooler now, and the grass smelled fresh as the crickets chirped around us. The back of the house was lit, casting an inviting glow over the lawn.

Walking past the pool, there was no sign of our adversaries. I hadn't realized how expansive the estate was, and I found the treed area beyond the formally landscaped yard bewitching. The moon shone overhead as the cicadas sang their distinctive song, beckoning us to join them.

Following close behind Ethan, I stayed silent while Jackson led us further into the woods. Chase was behind me, and if I looked back, I could still see the lights of the house. Large lights placed throughout the grounds provided uplighting in the treetops and ambient lighting in their immediate surround. But on the path, it was mostly dark apart from scattered beams of moonlight shining through the trees.

Jackson held up his hand, motioning us to stop. Based on the plan we had formulated earlier, Ethan and Jackson were to go one direction while Chase and I headed in another. This was the signal to split up, and Ethan looked back and winked at me before walking off with Jackson.

Out of the corner of my eye, I saw movement and aimed my gun. It beeped, and I had the gratification of hearing a grunt (which I assumed was Knox) confirming my hit. Chase looked at me wide-eyed. He probably assumed it was a lucky hit; I had no doubt the guys would be astonished to discover my shooting prowess. Never underestimate the lengths a paranoid father will go to keep his daughter safe, even if that means teaching her to shoot.

But before I could get too smug, my chest vibrated and my heart jolted. When my vest lit up, I gritted my teeth. *Crap*.

Dashing through the trees in the moonlight, the high-tech game of cat-and-mouse continued. It was exhilarating, and I could feel my skin glistening with sweat despite the cool air. It felt so good to jog and move; I had been aching to run again after my ankle injury.

Occasional volleys of fire were exchanged, alerting us of distant skirmishes. And each time one of us made a hit, Chase and I high-fived. I liked being on Chase's team; he made me feel protected while treating me like an equal. It almost felt like he wanted to see what I was capable of.

After a particularly strenuous pursuit, Chase and I stopped to catch our breath. A moment later, shots were fired, and Chase pulled me behind a tree. Leaning in so close our noses were almost touching, he whispered, "Stay here while I try to distract them; only run if you have to." At the feel of his warm breath against my skin, I shivered, focused just enough to absorb his instructions. If Chase distracted our enemy as well as he'd just dazed me, we'd win for sure.

Before I had a chance to respond, Chase raced off into the woods, firing as he ran. Suddenly left alone, I felt slightly bereft. So used to at least one of the guys around me at all times, I was surprised at how keenly I felt their absence in that moment.

When Chase didn't return after a few minutes, I crouched low and darted from tree to tree, trying to keep out of sight. Then, without warning, I heard a nearby voice call out, "Come out, come out, Haley." Another voice, "We know you're all alone;

we captured Chase." Wait, they could capture people?

As their playful taunts continued, I realized that the rival team was now circling me. I remained still, debating what to do. Hearing beeps whiz through the air at some unknown target, it was a shock when Jackson appeared next to me as if by magic. To say that I was impressed that he dodged them without getting hit was an understatement. He must have maneuvered through them with the stealth of a well-trained soldier.

Holding his gun in his right hand, Jackson swept me behind him with his left, creating a shield with his body. Instinctively, I turned my back to his, each of us facing out to meet the enemy. *I may be a damsel in distress, but I'm not going down without a fight.*

I felt his body shift and turned my head. A look passed between us as we shared a moment of camaraderie. For the first time, I felt like Jackson and I were on the same side.

Finger poised on the trigger, ready to spring at any sound, I waited for the impending ambush. I was able to make out a dark figure between the bushes and fired, my gun emitting the beeping noise I had become accustomed to. We hit two of our rivals before our vests made a funny noise that almost sounded like they were powering down.

I heard groans from the trees around us; Theo's voice rang out as he, Knox, Chase, and Liam emerged from the bushes. "Seriously? That went by way too fast."

I shook my head. "It's already over?" The ending felt almost anticlimactic after Jackson came to my rescue, and together, we fought off most of the opposing team.

Ethan appeared then, laughing as he wrapped an arm around my shoulder. "I guess that means you had fun."

After removing our gear and returning to the pool house, Jackson stood looking at his phone. "Ready for the run down?"

I wasn't sure what he was referring to, but all the guys nodded heads almost in unison. Jackson resumed talking. "Player hit the most times was Chase." One of the guys interjected a "womp womp," before Jackson said, "Player hit the least times was Knox."

Jackson scrolled down the screen with his finger. "The player with the most successful hits was me, with . . ." He paused and I saw his eyebrow raise a hair. "Haley in second."

Six distinct sets of eyes turned to stare at me.

Liam spoke first, his British accent taking on a slight twang. "Whoa there, Annie Oakley." I rolled my eyes and headed toward the kitchen while trying to hide my blush from the unexpected attention.

Ethan stood frozen, his hand hovering over a drink in the fridge. "So was that beginner's luck or . . ." and trailed off.

Realizing they were still staring at me expectantly, awaiting an explanation, I shrugged. "I know how to shoot a Glock 19; it wasn't that different."

I saw Theo's jaw drop before Knox patted me proudly on the shoulder. "I told you she's not like other girls."

I was puzzled by Knox's statement, but he seemed to intend it as a compliment. The rest of the guys apparently accepted my answer, at least for the moment, and moved around the pool house, grabbing drinks or popcorn.

With the exhilaration of the game wearing off and the chill of evening setting in, I rubbed my arms once to warm them. Before I could even ask for a blanket, Theo anticipated my need. "Here's a blanket for you." Theo threw it toward me, and in a funny, high pitched voice exclaimed, "It's so fluffy I'm gonna die!" The room erupted in laughter.

Watching *Despicable M*e, it became clear that his "fluffy" comment was a line from the movie. My cheeks were sore from smiling at the delightful movie, especially knowing the guys selected it specifically for me. Snuggled under a soft blanket between Chase and Knox, I was amazed by how at home I felt.

I glanced around the room, my eyes quickly running over Chase, Ethan, Theo, Liam, Jackson, and Knox. Individually, they were each so unique, but together, they were truly remarkable.

I thought back to what Ethan told me the night he shared my bed at the cabin. Sometimes home isn't a house or even family. Sometimes it's a group of friends who always have your back or finding a career you're passionate about.

Being here with them, I could actually see what Ethan meant. There was still a lot I didn't know about each of them, but it was clear that this group of guys had bonded through their broken backgrounds and had redefined home in their own terms.

I tried to ignore the longing settling over me. Although I currently had a roof over my head, I was still without a home. And as comfortable as I felt in that moment, I knew my time here—with the six of them—was fleeting.

Despite our emerging friendships, I knew I was an obligation, the byproduct of a botched assignment. My heart ached at the thought that a day would come when I would part ways with the guys, but I had to put my dad, and myself, first.

I held out hope that my dad was just biding his time until it was safe to reappear. In the meantime, I was determined to do everything I could to find him. I would continue to enjoy my time in Santa Cruz, but I wouldn't be able to relax until I knew he was okay.

Thinking back to my birthday, I laughed to myself. So much had changed in a few short weeks, I barely recognized my life. I went from living in almost complete solitude to constantly being surrounded. It was as unfamiliar as it was comforting. I had no idea what the next few months would bring, but for the first time, I was demanding a say in my life and my future.

Zenith: San Jose, California

Jackson answered the incoming call: "Good morning, Uncle. How are you?"

Uncle: "I'm good, Jax. Sorry to call so early, but I'm in D.C., and I have a meeting in half an hour. I just wanted to check in before the week started."

Jackson: "Thanks again for letting us stay at your house this weekend. I think there was only a few thousand dollars' worth of damage this time."

Uncle: Laughing, "Of course. You know you're welcome any time; it will always be your home." He paused. "Status?"

Jackson: "The Hamlet project wrapped up successfully. Theo and Liam are making progress on Gandalf, and Finch is close to completion. We are still searching for Phoenix's dad, Brian Taylor. We connected our client, Gerald Douglas, to his disappearance, but we are still trying to discern Douglas's motives."

Uncle: "Good. Any questions or concerns?"

Jackson: "No questions, but I am concerned with how attached several members of the team are getting to Phoenix."

Uncle: "Well, that's not that surprising, but you need to make sure she's not a distraction for your team."

Jackson: "Trust me, I know. Since one of us has to be with her at all times, I had a talk with the team Friday night. Everyone agreed that none of us will pursue her romantically."

Uncle: "Do you think that will work?"

Jackson: "I hope so, but I honestly don't know; several of them seem very invested. I'm just hoping to get her out of the picture before it becomes an issue."

Uncle: "What's your game plan?"

Jackson: "Phoenix is starting work today. And fortunately, we received a message that Mr. Douglas wants to hire Zenith as private security for his fundraiser at the end of the month. Hopefully this will be what we need to find Brian Taylor."

Uncle: "Perfect. Keep me updated."

A Note from Autumn Reed & Julia Clarke

Thank you so much for reading *Phoenix*! If you enjoyed the book, we would truly appreciate it if you would share your thoughts by writing a review on Amazon. To learn more about us and The Stardust Series, please visit our website or contact us at authors@autumnandjulia.com.

Also, don't forget to sign up for our newsletter for sneak peeks, behind-the-scenes details, and upcoming releases!

XO,
Autumn + Julia

Draco (Book Two of The Stardust Series)
Available now!

It's been two weeks since Haley Jones turned eighteen and her life was turned upside down. While searching for her dad, Haley is adjusting to life in Santa Cruz with a new job and friends. Surrounded by six dangerously appealing guys, she's still trying to figure out just who Liam, Knox, Ethan, Chase, Theo, and Jackson are and what they do. From a twenty-first birthday party to a swanky costume gala, Haley discovers just how difficult it can be to fit in and that maybe it's okay to stand out.

About the Authors

Autumn and Julia met at work and bonded over their mutual love of historic homes, photography, and good books. While they didn't plan on co-authoring a novel, what started as daydreaming transformed into brainstorming and then actual writing.

Together, Autumn and Julia make the perfect pair, balancing impulsive with indecisive and attention to detail with an eye for the big picture. Despite their different personalities, Autumn and Julia share a common vision in their writing and love bouncing ideas off each other. They see the creative process as a challenge, a game, and delight in living in a world of their own creation.

Printed in Poland
by Amazon Fulfillment
Poland Sp. z o.o., Wrocław